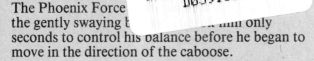

## Calvin Jam...
## from the bri...

The Phoenix Force ... the gently swaying ... him only seconds to control his balance before he began to move in the direction of the caboose.

With his arms held straight out from his sides, James jumped across the space between one boxcar to the next. He was sure that both cars were packed with heroin from the mountain opium refinery.

As James knelt and leaned out over the edge of the car, the train unexpectedly listed to the left, throwing him back and then forward while he compensated for the abrupt shifting of his weight. His head hung between the two cars for a fraction of a second—a second that was long enough for the Thai gunman who stood down below to whip his submachine gun into the air. And long enough for him to blast away.

**Mack Bolan's**
# PHOENIX FORCE

# PHOENIX FORCE

# Slow Death

## Gar Wilson

A GOLD EAGLE BOOK FROM

# WORLDWIDE

TORONTO • NEW YORK • LONDON • PARIS
AMSTERDAM • STOCKHOLM • HAMBURG
ATHENS • MILAN • TOKYO • SYDNEY

First edition March 1987

ISBN 0-373-61328-8

Special thanks and acknowledgment to
Paul Glen Neuman for his contribution to this work.

Printed in Canada

**1**

Richard Warren opened his eyes and wondered where he was. He was lying in the dark with a skull-splitting pain in his head.

Gingerly his fingers probed the sore area on the back of his head. Even in the dim light he could see that his fingers were covered with blood. He gasped and quickly closed his eyes, fighting against the tide of nausea rising in his throat.

He took a deep breath and the queasiness subsided. Another deep breath and he opened his eyes again. Overhead a low-wattage bulb stared at him through the fine wire mesh of a screen. How long had he been unconscious, he wondered.

He blinked and raised his left hand to check the time. He tugged at his sleeve. His wrist was bare.

''The bastards took it,'' a man's voice above and behind Warren announced. ''Your watch, your wallet and even your car keys if you had any. Everything.''

Warren spread the fingers of his left hand and saw that even his wedding ring was missing.

"See?" the unseen person said. "What did I tell you? They didn't leave anything. They took it all."

"Bessell, is that you?" Warren asked, thinking he recognized the voice.

"Yeah, it's me," Bessell confirmed. "And Lou Grenhof and old Harry Wheeler are here with us, too. Lou's about the same as you, but Harry's just plain out of it. Somebody sapped him pretty damn hard. I don't know if he'll ever wake up. Looks to me he's leaking more on the floor than blood, if you know what I mean."

Warren tried to sit and Bessell's hands gripped him by the shoulders, helping him up.

"Steady now," Bessell advised. "They didn't whack you on the head as hard as they did Harry, but the bump you're sporting runs a close second. How are you feeling?"

As Warren sat up his world started to swim. Then the dizziness ebbed away, and he was all right.

"Better now?" Bessell asked.

Warren nodded carefully. "I'll live. Where the hell are we?"

"Bang Kwang." Lou Grenhof spoke for the first time. "They've thrown us into Bang Kwang."

"The prison?" Warren's abrupt query betrayed his shock. "But why?"

"We were hoping you could tell us," Grenhof said.

"Not me," Warren returned, shaking his head.

The cell they were in was not much larger than a walk-in closet. Three of its walls were of rough-textured concrete, while the entire fourth side, facing onto a dimly lit corridor, consisted of closely spaced vertical bars with a metal door hinged into the bars on the right. Except for the cell's four occupants, it was empty.

"So we're in the prison," Warren continued, feeling strong enough to stand. "Without so much as a pot to piss in. That's a good sign."

"How's that?" Grenhof asked.

"Easy," Warren explained to the younger Drug Enforcement Agency operative. "If the Thai authorities intended to hold us for any length of time, they'd have given us more comfortable accommodations, toilet facilities at least, even if just a bucket. The fact that they dumped us in here means our stay's going to be short."

"Not for Harry," Grenhof muttered.

Warren crossed to where Harry Wheeler lay sprawled on his back on the dirty floor of the cell and knelt to look at him. Bessell's diagnosis of the older man's injuries was not far from the truth. Sticky matter had leaked from a wound on Wheeler's skull, and his breathing was shallow.

"At least he's still breathing," Warren said.

"But for how long?" Grenhof countered anxiously. "If Harry doesn't see a doctor soon, we can write him off."

"This is crazy!" Bessell complained. "There's absolutely no reason for us to be in here."

"Obviously somebody made a mistake," Warren said.

"With all *four* of us?" Bessell shook his head. "Be serious. We're not talking about a simple clerical error. We're in Bang Kwang because someone wanted us here."

"But who?" Grenhof voiced the question they were all thinking. "Where were you guys when you got hit?"

"I was coming out of the Miami," Bessell replied, referring to a hotel in the Sukhumvit area of Bangkok that was favored by foreigners, particularly Arab tourists. "I was to meet one of my regular informants there, but the little runt never showed."

"And you got hit when you left, just as you got into your car?" Warren asked.

"Yeah." Bessell looked at Warren and nodded. "I had the key in the lock and was opening the door when the ceiling caved in on me. The scenario sound familiar?"

"Close to it," Warren confirmed. "Only my meeting was set for the Golden Horse Hotel on Dumrongrak Road. My contact didn't show either, though it's not the first time that's happened. I waited thirty minutes before calling it quits."

"Which is about how long it took me to decide my meeting at the Blue Fox was a bust," Grenhof chimed in.

"Who were you supposed to meet?" Bessell asked.

"You know him," Grenhof answered. "Sutha Nakhon."

"That son of a bitch," Warren said. "My meeting was with Sutha, too."

"And mine." Bessell made it unanimous. "Let's face it, gentlemen, Sutha set us up. We've been had."

"And I'll bet that goes for Harry, too," Warren concluded. "Sutha suckered us all into the same trap."

"Well, he'd better be on his way out of Thailand right now," Bessell said. "Because, if I catch up to him when I get out, he's history. How long do you guys figure we've been in here, anyway?"

Warren shrugged. "Three or four hours, more or less," he answered. "How long was I unconscious after you came to?"

"I woke up first, then Grenhof," Bessell said. "You didn't come around for another hour or so."

"Okay," Warren said. "It was going on eight when I got hit. Transportation to the prison wouldn't take long. Offhand, I'd say it's somewhere between midnight and one in the morning right now."

"Sounds likely," Bessell said. "I've questioned prisoners here at Bang Kwang, and it's noisy as hell during the day. But the prison's pretty damn quiet now." He pressed his face to the bars and scanned up and down the corridor as best he could. "I can see a couple of doors, but they're closed with no windows. And I don't see any other cells, either. We're in an isolation area of some kind."

"Which brings us back to my original conviction," Warren reminded them. "Given the lack of facilities, our stay here is obviously meant to be short. Besides, even if that wasn't what they had in mind, the latest they can keep us locked up is tomorrow noon. You both know if we fail to check in by midmorning the rest of our team will send out the bloodhounds to find us."

"Maybe," Grenhof said. "All the same, I'd rather not wait that long."

"What I don't understand," Bessell pointed out, "is why Sutha went to such lengths to put us in here. Were either of you about to break open something big?"

Warren and Grenhof shook their heads.

"Neither was I," Bessell went on. "It's been quiet for me lately. Cut and dried. I could have photocopied my Monday report and used it the rest of the week. It's been that slow."

Bessell stopped talking as the door at the left end of the corridor creaked open. The three DEA men tensed. Bessell tried again to look down the hall.

"Well?" Grenhof demanded as the shuffling sound of sandals reached their ears. "Who is it?"

But before Bessell could answer the man was there. He was an ancient Burmese, much older than the Americans and very thin. The faded cotton pajama pants he wore were held up by a string tied around his waist. Strapped over the old man's right shoulder was a wooden box that looked like a cooler. Its weight tilted him to one side as if he were about to topple over.

Without saying a word the Burmese convict shuffled to a halt in front of the cell and with difficulty lowered his cargo to the floor. He squatted, joints creaking, and flipped open the lid of the box. It was lined with Styrofoam insulation and contained several white cardboard cartons. He removed four of these then closed the lid again.

The bars of the cell were just far enough apart for him to pass the cartons through and put them on the floor. Bessell bent and picked up one of them. It was warm. He held it to his nose.

"Food," he told the others.

Still not speaking, the Burmese prisoner adjusted the strap of the insulated box over his right shoulder and, bracing his feet, stood with his cumbersome burden. Giving the Americans a toothless grin, he started down the corridor.

"Hey, wait!" Grenhof pushed Bessell aside and waved his arms through the bars as he shouted after the old man. "Don't go yet. We need a doctor. Tell the guards we're awake and want to talk. We want to talk to a guard!"

But if the old man understood English, or even heard Grenhof's plaintive cry for help, he showed no sign. While Grenhof gesticulated and shouted, the convict who had brought the food disappeared through the door at the end of the hallway. Grenhof rested his forehead against the bars and sighed.

"Damn!"

"Don't let it get to you," Bessell said, handing Grenhof a food carton. "At least they're not starving us to death. Here."

Reluctantly Grenhof accepted the container. "It looks like what they used to sell goldfish in when I was a kid."

Bessell held out another box to Warren. "Who said that cartons for goldfish ever went out of style?" He hooked his thumbs under the lid of his own food container. "Whatever it is, though, we'd better eat it. We can't be sure when we'll be fed again."

Bessell tore open the lid and peered hopefully inside at a small helping of plain boiled rice. He scooped some into his mouth with his fingers, then chewed and swallowed the cooked grain. "Bland, but edible," he announced.

Warren sampled the rice and agreed. "I've had worse."

"What the hell's wrong with you two?" In a fit of anger Grenhof bounced his box of rice off the rear wall of the cell, the content's scattering everywhere. "We're in Bangkok's pride and joy, Bang Kwang prison, not at a Sunday barbecue in the park."

Warren shook his head in disapproval. "Take it easy, Grenhof. Bessell and I know the facts without having to hear them from you. Throwing a tantrum like a spoiled two-year-old isn't going to solve anything. Just settle down."

Grenhof looked as if he were going to tell Warren where he could stuff his remarks, then he changed his mind and stretched out his hands to Warren. "Sorry, Richard. Guilty as charged. I'm feeling claustrophobic, that's all. I've never liked being inside *any* enclosed space. Sorry."

"Ah, forget it," Warren said, picking up the last food package and handing it to Grenhof. "Harry's in no condition to enjoy this, so you may as well eat it."

Grenhof accepted the container of rice without further complaint. "Yeah, sure, Warren. Thanks."

Then they heard the door at the end of the corridor open again.

"What now?" Grenhof wondered aloud.

"Maybe it's our waiter with the wine list," Bessell said with a grin.

Bessell was wrong. Their latest visitor was a Buddhist monk clothed in the yellow robe of his faith. He paused before their cell and raised his hands as though in prayer. Then he began to speak softly and very rapidly in Thai. Less than a minute later, he offered the three American prisoners another *wai*, the prayerlike gesture he had started with, then quickly made his departure.

Grenhof had to restrain himself from calling after the saffron-robed monk. He absently licked a few grains of rice from his fingers as a chill of dread struck deep between his shoulder blades.

"I don't like it, guys," Grenhof finally said. "First the rice, and now a monk shows up. What do you make of it?"

"Food for the body and for the soul," Bessell answered, not caring for the direction the conversation was taking.

"Yeah?" Grenhof was far from convinced. "Well, a final meal and a blessing by Father Flannigan is more how I read it."

"Ridiculous!" Richard Warren also thought Grenhof was exaggerating. Sutha Nakhon, the Thai informant who was somehow connected with their predicament, was obviously indulging himself with some joke at their expense. Whatever Sutha's reason for booking them a room at the Bang Kwang Hilton, Warren had no doubt the scheming informant's motives would soon come to light. "Like I said before, Grenhof…take it easy. You're blowing this thing way out of proportion."

Grenhof jerked his thumb at their unconscious associate on the floor. "Tell that to Harry."

"No," Bessell protested, "Richard's right. If you don't mind, Grenhof, keep your unhealthy opinions to yourself."

Grenhof shook an accusing finger in Bessell's direction. "You'll see."

Both Bessell and Warren were silently praying Grenhof was wrong when the corridor door opened for the third time. A five-man squad of prison guards marched into view and came to a halt in front of the cell. Four of the guards were armed with automatic rifles. The fifth unfolded and looked at a piece of paper.

"I am here for Richard Warren," he announced in Thai-accented English.

"That's me," Warren said, stepping forward. "Thank goodness you speak English. I don't know what the devil's going on, but somebody on your end's got their wires crossed. We've been beaten, abducted, our personal effects have been stolen, and we've been thrown into this cell without any justification." He pointed to the unconscious Harry Wheeler. "This man is seriously injured and needs medical attention, and I demand to know what's going to be done about it, or so help me, heads are going to—"

"Silence!" the guard ordered. At his signal, one of the rifle-bearing men unlocked the barred door to the cell. "You, Richard Warren, will come with me now."

The DEA agent balked. "Where to? Where are you taking me?"

The guard in charge came nearer and said, "Do not make me send my men in to get you. I assure you it would not be a pleasant experience for you or your friends."

Warren held up his hands as the armed guards began to advance. "All right, hold it right there, I get the picture. What about a doctor for my friend?"

"He will be taken care of," the guard promised, smiling like a baby shark after its first taste of blood. "You have my word."

Warren exchanged nervous glances with Grenhof and Bessell. "You guys hang tight. They're probably taking me to see someone higher on the totem pole than these clowns. I'll take care of things, don't worry. Once they realize their mistake we'll be out of here in no time flat."

"Good luck," Bessell said.

"Yeah," Grenhof added. "We're depending on you, Warren. Don't let us down."

"Never," Warren vowed, stepping into the corridor. Three of the rifle-toting Thais kept their weapons trained on him, while the one who had opened the cell now locked it again with the jarring clang of metal striking metal.

Warren did his best to appear confident as he turned to his left. "All right. Let's go."

The number-one guard folded the piece of paper and tucked it into his breast pocket. "Not that way," he said. "Follow me."

With the English-speaking Thai in the lead and the four remaining guards flanking their prisoner, Warren was herded down the corridor and through the door at the end. They entered a poorly lit hallway much like the one they had left behind.

Richard Warren walked unafraid. All he needed was the opportunity to explain to a prison official with clout that he and his associates didn't belong locked up in Bang Kwang. Surely, he reasoned, someone in the prison would be willing to listen to the facts.

They came to a short stone stairway, at the bottom of which was a solid steel door with a black ring of iron hanging from its center. The word *dungeon* sprang to Warren's mind. The Thai guard in the lead knocked once and the door was opened from within.

"God, no!" Warren said with a gasp as he was ushered through the doorway.

The long narrow room they entered resembled an indoor shooting range. The wall at the far end was lined with sandbags, and ten feet in front of it a wooden cross-shaped support was embedded in the floor. At the nearer end of the room, resting upon a four-legged stand, was a Blackmann machine gun, its dark dull barrel aimed in the direction of the sand-bagged wall. Next to the Blackmann was someone Warren recognized—Police Corporal Pratom Arpa-sat. The American's legs went rubbery…and his knees threatened to buckle. Police Corporal Pratom Arpa-sat was Bang Kwang prison's chief executioner.

"No, wait," Warren protested, resisting in vain as he was dragged toward the cross-shaped support. His arms were stretched wide, and his wrists were mana-cled to the cross. When the guards moved away he was facing the wall of sandbags, his back to Pratom Ar-pasat.

"You're making a terrible mistake," Warren in-sisted, craning his neck around as far as he could. "I'm a special officer with the United States Drug Enforcement Agency stationed here in Thailand. So are the other three men you have locked up in this stinking prison, you bastard!''

He struggled to free himself, but the manacles held him fast. ''You can't kill us all and get away with it! It'll never happen. We're on your side, you son of a bitch.''

''Are you finished?'' the police corporal inquired. When Warren failed to answer, the Thai policeman continued. ''You, Richard Warren, have been found guilty of committing crimes against the people of Thailand. For these willful offenses you have been sentenced to die.''

''What have I done? Tell me what I have done.'' Numb almost to the point of insensibility, Warren could no longer offer resistance as a guard tied a blindfold over his eyes. Tears trickled down his cheeks. A tremor of fear rippled through him from head to toe.

Pratom Arpasat's Buddhist religion prohibited killing any defenseless being. But the wily Thai police corporal was not to be thwarted. While the prisoner waited for the inevitable, one of the guards inserted a board in a rectangular slot in the floor, midway between the machine gun and the cross Richard Warren was fastened to.

The wood plank would enable Pratom Arpasat to perform his task without violating the precepts of his religion. When it was time for the DEA agent to die, the executioner would simply aim the Blackmann at the board. That Richard Warren was in the direct line

of fire was only a coincidence, a convenient solution
to the police corporal's dilemma.

The guard who had inserted the plank quickly
backed out of danger to join the others behind the
Blackmann. Pratom Arpasat nodded and took his
place at the gun.

"Goodbye, Richard Warren," he said. "Your time
is truly now."

Before Warren could turn his head to plead once
again for mercy the executioner opened fire, the powerful Blackmann machine gun filling the room with
thunder. The board in the slot was destroyed instantly. So was Richard Warren. In a heartbeat the
helpless DEA agent made the journey from life to
death.

The police corporal moved away from the Blackmann and observed his handiwork, more than satisfied with the results.

"Very good," he commented, then issued instructions to the guard who had led Richard Warren to his
doom. "Remove the body and bring me the next prisoner."

**2**

Hal Brognola shoved his hands deeper into the pockets of his overcoat as he stood beside the Stony Man Farm helipad waiting for the president's helicopter to land. The skies over Virginia's Blue Ridge Mountains were heavy with somber gray clouds. The air was freezer-cold, and burned the lungs when inhaled. The snowstorm the National Weather Bureau had promised all week would hit before dark.

A personal visit from the president of the United States did not strike the country's foremost federal agent as unusual. Brognola was accustomed to regular interaction with America's commander-in-chief. What did strike Brognola as odd was that he had learned of the president's impending visit to Stony Man Farm less than twenty minutes before. Such an unscheduled stopover could mean only one thing: somewhere within the global community trouble was brewing.

Stony Man Farm had been created to cope with subversion in its ugliest forms. The men of Phoenix Force and Able Team, the crack antiterrorist squads directed by Brognola, were qualified and ready to meet any challenge. If the president had a problem, Stony Man Farm held the solution.

Brognola shielded his eyes as the president's CH-53 helicopter swept into view and gracefully touched down. The Super Jolly's rotors gradually stopped turning. Seconds later Brognola was shaking the president's hand.

Brognola escorted the president into his office. The head Fed resisted the urge to chew on one of his ubiquitous cigars as he listened to what the president had to say.

"I kept close tabs on that Vatican business," the president began, "and the assignment in Mongolia. I think that one wound up in Hong Kong, right?"

"That's right, sir," Brognola confirmed. "Two rough assignments, one right after the other."

"My sources told me that a couple of your men got hurt," the president commented. "Your report didn't give details about the injuries, but another intel source suggests they were tortured."

"They're all fit for duty now, sir," Brognola assured him. "They were injured during the incident at the Vatican and were fully recovered for the Mongolian assignment."

"Okay," the president said with a nod. "I won't worry about the condition of your men. I certainly can't argue with the results. But I understand you've brought in a couple of extra men to help on missions. Are you sure they're suited to this sort of thing?"

"Absolutely," the Fed responded with a poker player's smile. "Only the best belong to Phoenix Force, and only the best work with them. That's only fair. And given the nature of a typical Phoenix Force assignment, it's wise to have understudies waiting in the wings."

"I know," the president said. "The show must go on, isn't that how it goes?"

"Right. And if we're not ready to perform each time the curtain rises, the audience doesn't get its money back. What do you have for us this time, sir?"

The president leaned forward and frowned. "I'm not really sure. We could have a showstopper on our hands, or something that closes on opening night. In any case, I'm talking about something that's just happened in Bangkok."

"Involving the Thai government?"

"Much closer to home, I'm afraid. You're aware, of course, that we have a substantial number of DEA special agents stationed in Thailand."

"Yes," Brognola replied. "Close to twenty-one at last count, unless I'm mistaken."

"At this time yesterday your estimate would have been correct. Unfortunately, that number has now been savagely reduced to seventeen. Four of our DEA agents have been murdered."

"Murdered?" Brognola repeated. "Do we have any idea who's behind the killings?"

"We do," the president said, "but that's where what we know of the incident starts falling apart. The

four Americans were executed in Bangkok's Bang
Kwang prison. Preliminary information indicates that
all four were beaten prior to their deaths, one of them
severely so. They were incarcerated on trumped-up
charges and were executed by order of a Thai court
document that ultimately proved to be a forgery. Naturally, under the circumstances, the remaining seventeen DEA personnel are fearful for their lives.''

"Who can blame them?" Brognola observed.
"From the sound of things, any one of the agents
could have been singled out for the party at Bang
Kwang prison. Have any subsequent attempts been
made on their lives?''

"None as yet," the president replied. "And that's
how we'd like to keep it. From what I've been told, the
DEA people in Bangkok are just as much in the dark
over this as we are.''

"What has been the response from the Thai government?''

"About what you would expect. Shock, remorse
and profuse denial that they had anything to do with
having our men killed. Frankly, Hal, I'm inclined to
believe them. The Thai government has enough on its
plate already without searching around for this kind
of indigestion.''

"I would think they'd still be counting their losses
after that latest coup attempt," Brognola said. "How
many does that make now? Something like eighteen of
them since 1932.''

"Which is why I believe the Thai government is innocent of these murders," the president insisted. "They're too busy rebuilding to willingly throw a snag like this in the way of reconstruction."

"Well, if that's the case," Brognola said, "the identity of those responsible for the murders is on the open market. Anybody and his brother could be behind the killings."

"Precisely," agreed the president. "And that's why I want Phoenix Force sent to Thailand. If anyone can make sense of this mess, they can."

"I'm sure they appreciate your confidence in them, Mr. President."

"They've earned that confidence, Hal. And my respect. I don't know what kind of situation is cooking in Thailand. Whatever it is, I want Phoenix Force to get to the bottom of it, to make sure the show over there closes early. I know they'll give a good performance."

"They will because they're just like you, sir," Hal Brognola promised. "They hate bad reviews."

**3**

The bar was empty when the four men entered.

"Don't step in that puddle of water," one warned.

"It's not water," the next man in the door insisted.

"I knew it . . . the place is a regular *cagadero*," the third man told the first.

"It certainly does have an air about it," decided the fourth man.

The interior of the Luva Brewski tavern had seen better days. And better decades. The bar's dank atmosphere combined the ripe odors of mildew, flat beer and faulty plumbing. The murky gloom was lightened inadequately by yellow bulbs, not much larger than cherry tomatoes, hidden within dirty brown lampshades that decorated the ceiling like miniature parachutes.

A lone pool table collected dust in a corner, its playing surface covered by crates of beer and soft drink empties. A moose head hung lopsided on the wall above a jukebox silently begging for change.

The four men took a seat at the table farthest from the entrance. There was no bartender in sight.

"Well, gents," David McCarter said, rubbing his palms together in anticipation, "what's your pleasure?"

Gary Manning looked at his British friend and answered with true sincerity. "How about four bottles of oxygen? You buy."

"Leave off," the cockney protested. "It's not as bad as all that."

"David's right," Rafael Encizo put in. "It's worse."

"See?" Manning nodded at McCarter. "Nobody but you would consider this dump suitable for human habitation."

"Not so fast." McCarter brightened, indicating the lanky black American sitting opposite him. "We haven't heard from Calvin on the subject."

"Trust Gary on this one," Calvin James counseled, nodding toward the brawny Canadian next to McCarter. "The Luva Brewski's a dive."

"The trouble with you, mates, is you've let a pampered life-style corrupt you. You've lost your sense of adventure."

"Some adventures I can do without," Manning said. "Why don't we wait for our flight out of Detroit at the airport? It's everything the Luva Brewski isn't—warm, comfortable and clean."

Just then a balding man in his mid-to-late fifties appeared through a curtained-off doorway behind the bar. He wore a lime-green pullover vest with matching bow tie, and a dingy-white shirt with rolled-up sleeves. His forearms, unlike his scalp, were hairy.

Humming softly to himself he picked up a damp towel and began wiping off the bar. Obviously he was the bartender. His humming became a whistle, and finally he burst into song, his cloth sweeping this way and that in time to the music.

"Excuse me?" McCarter called to get his attention.

"What!" The man started and clutched his hands to his chest. "You nearly gave me a heart attack. Why didn't you tell me you were here?"

"That's what I was trying to do," McCarter said.

"From out of town, huh?" the bartender commented, picking up on McCarter's British accent. "The Luva Brewski doesn't get many tourists."

"I can't imagine why not," Manning said.

"I said tourists, bub, not customers. Customers I got coming out my ears."

"Yeah, we noticed how we had to fight our way in," James said.

"That's 'cause you're here before the rush," the indignant bartender shot back. "A few more minutes and this joint'll be wall-to-wall people."

"Then we'd better place our order now," Encizo said, laughing. "While we can still enjoy your undivided attention."

The bartender raised his eyebrows. "What's this, another foreigner? Damn! Ain't any of you guys American?"

James raised his hand. "Me."

"What about you?" the bald man asked Manning.

"Canadian," Manning said. "Now, about our drinks."

"Yeah, yeah," the bartender said. "Four brewskis on tap, coming right up."

"If it's all the same to you," Manning said, "I'll take mine in a bottle."

Encizo and James chimed in, "Me too," and the bartender frowned.

"Any special reason you fellas don't want your beer on tap?" he asked.

Manning trailed his finger through the layer of dust on their table. "Because they sterilize the bottles before they put the beer in."

The bartender considered the response, then answered, "Well, sure, I guess they do."

"Then that's all the reason you need," Manning told him.

"What about the Brit?"

"I'll have a can of Coca-Cola Classic, thanks," McCarter replied. "Ice cold, if possible."

"I think I can handle it," the bartender returned. "A can of Coke and three bottles of beer. Domestic brands for you fellas?"

"Wrong again," Manning said. "Make mine a Molson Golden."

"Dos Equis for me," Encizo said.

"And I'll have a Heineken." James was the last to order.

Muttering something about "foreigners" in a stage whisper, the bartender opened the cooler behind the bar and removed three bottles and a can of Coca-Cola Classic, which he banged down on the bar.

"Here you go," he announced. "Three imports and a can of soda pop."

"What?" Manning exclaimed. "You're not bringing the drinks to our table?"

"Nope." The bartender adjusted his bow tie and smiled. "You change your mind and order domestic, well, that's another story. Stick with the imports, and how you get your drinks is your business."

"But Coke is bottled in the United States," McCarter pointed out.

"So are plenty of fine domestic beers," replied the bartender. "Are you paying for the imports, or not? I got to know now. Any minute and it's going to be—"

"Wall-to-wall people." McCarter completed the bald man's sentence. "We already heard." The Englishman pushed back his chair and sauntered to the bar. "We certainly don't want to get caught in the rush."

"You're the kind of guy who makes me glad I never got to England, fella," the bartender said as McCarter paid him for the drinks.

"That makes two of us, guv."

The tavern's front door opened and a gust of freezing Detroit winter wind blew in. So did a half dozen thirsty workers who had just ended their shift on the assembly line at the automobile plant across the street.

Spying the newcomers, the bartender reached immediately for an empty glass and lifted it to a nearby spigot. McCarter carried the bottles and his can of Coca-Cola Classic to the table the Phoenix Force members were sharing.

Raised in London's tough East End, David McCarter was a veteran of Great Britain's Strategic Air Service. A superb pistol marksman, an expert pilot and a master of virtually every form of combat, the cockney commando had seen action in Hong Kong and Oman. In 1980 he had participated in Operation Nimrod, the successful SAS raid on the Iranian embassy in London.

Though often short-tempered and high-strung when not being challenged in battle, the fox-faced Briton, fearless in the face of danger, was one of the finest antiterrorists in the world.

McCarter set the drinks on their table as six more autoworkers pushed their way into the tavern. The bartender flashed the Londoner and his friends an "I told you so" look as he began passing out glasses of draft beer as fast as he could fill them.

"Well, what do you know?" Gary Manning mused, twisting off the cap of his Molson Golden. "The guy was telling the truth."

The barrel-chested Canadian was the top sniper on the Phoenix Force team, and one of the world's foremost experts in explosives and demolition. Those who had seen him in action swore Gary Manning could blast the stamp off an envelope without harming the letter inside.

Following a stint in the Canadian army as a special observer with the Fifth Special Forces in Vietnam, Manning had joined the Royal Canadian Mounted Police's counterterrorist division. He had worked in Europe in conjunction with the crack GSG-9 antiterrorist unit in West Germany.

When the RCMP quit playing the espionage game, Manning said no to the boredom of a desk job and moved into the private sector as a security expert with North America International. Between Phoenix Force missions, Manning, a workaholic, still found time to put his considerable skills to work for the company.

On behalf of NAI, Manning had spent the past week in Motor City beefing up security at a pharmaceutical research facility. Medical research in the U.S. was big business. A single breakthrough in the industry could be worth millions of dollars, and the constant threat of industrial espionage made security a major concern.

Manning had invited his friends to join him in Detroit when his assignment ended, to fly north together for some hunting and relaxation at a cabin in Churchill, Manitoba.

By now the bartender was working at top speed to keep up with the spate of customers. Several of the autoworkers retired to tables with their drinks, others just leaned on the bar. Someone fed money into the jukebox, and a toe-tapping country song about broken hearts and empty promises began to play.

"Hey, man," Calvin James announced as the singer launched into an upbeat chorus. "That's Charley Pride. They used to play his songs over AFR all the time in Nam."

The long road that led Calvin James into the ranks of Phoenix Force began in a poverty-stricken neighborhood on the South Side of Chicago, where the hard realities of urban survival were a way of life. By the time he was twelve, the lanky black youth was adept at protecting himself with fists, feet and an occasional razor or knife.

At age seventeen Calvin enlisted in the U.S. Navy, where he was trained as a hospital corpsman. This led to a two-year tour of duty in Vietnam with the SEALS. Wounded during his final sortie, he was decorated for valor and honorably discharged.

Conditions back home in Chicago had not improved during James's absence. Both his mother and sister were the innocent victims of brutal crimes that were threatening to erode the very foundation of American society.

James had been studying medicine and chemistry at UCLA, but shortly after his sister was buried, he switched to police science. Following graduation he joined the San Francisco Police Department, gaining further law-enforcement experience with the city's SWAT team.

The song on the Luva Brewski's jukebox ended and another began, a ballad about an assembly-line auto-worker building a car at home with parts he steals one at a time. The crowd cheered each time the chorus came around. Beer was flowing like a flood, and the stale air in the bar was hazy with tobacco smoke.

"I'd hate to be here on a Saturday night," Encizo commented loud enough to be heard over the music. "These cowboys look like they could be rowdy if they put their minds to it."

The Cuban considered himself to be one of the luckiest members of Phoenix Force. Felled by an enemy bullet during the team's clash with ODESSA Nazis in France, Encizo's near-fatal head wound had sidelined him for four recent missions. The inactivity during his convalescence had nearly driven him crazy.

During Castro's push to shackle Cuba with the chains of communism, Rafael had lost his father, mother and older brother to execution squads. His two sisters and younger brother had been abducted and taken to Cuba's new centers for higher learning—brain mills whose only purpose was to implant the glories of Marxism and the socialist revolution within fertile young minds.

Opposing the injustice of the Castro regime and the Communist takeover of his country, Encizo had participated in the ill-fated Bay of Pigs invasion in 1961. Captured and held in El Principe, the infamous prison Castro's political opponents called home, Encizo was a prime target for reeducation by the Russian "technicians.'' If they could break the will of one as obstinate as Encizo, they reasoned, they could manipulate the beliefs of anyone. Encizo went along with their game. He endured their torture then allowed himself to snap before his captors' eyes. He became a model prisoner. One desperate afternoon his good behavior paid off. A guard was careless. Encizo broke the man's neck and escaped.

In the United States, Encizo became a naturalized citizen and put the horrors of the past behind him. He worked as a treasure hunter, a diving instructor and a professional bodyguard. When asked to join Phoenix Force he had been an insurance investigator for maritime claims.

Encizo sighed with relief as McCarter drained the last of his Coke and lowered the empty can to the table.

"Finally," he said. "Now can we leave?"

"You guys haven't finished your beer," McCarter said.

"We can buy more at the airport," Manning responded. "We can also breathe air there that hasn't been filtered through smoke or sewage. The Luva Brewski's giving me a headache."

McCarter shrugged. "Oh, all right, but just see if I go out of my way to pick a nice place to wet our whistles next time."

"That's a promise I'll hold you to," Manning replied.

The country singer stopped in the middle of his song. Someone shouted in complaint and someone else told the complainer to shut up. A hush fell over the crowd as the Luva Brewski patrons turned their attention on the Phoenix Force table.

"I think maybe we should have ordered domestic," James muttered above the sudden silence.

"Out of my way," a booming voice bellowed from the direction of the bar. The customers crowding the floor shifted to the left and right, permitting the bellower to be seen.

Built like an upright freezer, with fists the size of ice blocks, he ambled across the floor. Clutched in the bruiser's right paw was a schooner of beer.

"We have a plane to catch," Manning reminded McCarter. "So behave yourself."

"Don't I always?" the British commando asked innocently.

"Please," Manning told him. "If I start laughing now these guys will really get steamed."

McCarter noted that several of the men in the crowd were swaying on their feet. "Looks like some of them are already pissed."

"Just behave yourself," Manning repeated.

"Trust me," McCarter said.

Manning groaned to himself.

Then the hulk arrived at their table and loomed over them like a small mountain of flesh. His belly drooped over his belt, dark circles of sweat stained his shirt beneath his arms. He sounded like an engine in need of tuning when he breathed. He placed his ham-sized left hand on the back of McCarter's chair and lowered the half-empty schooner of beer to the table.

"Excuse me, mate," McCarter said, having no difficulty being heard since the bar now was quiet enough to hear a keg drop. "Illumination within this establishment being what it isn't, I would thank you to cease eclipsing our little conversation here."

The upright freezer frowned. "Huh?"

"You're blocking our light," McCarter said.

"Oh, that." The man bobbed his blockish head up and down, much to the approval of his friends. "Too bad."

"I see," McCarter said, smiling. "Well, if you don't care to be civil about it, would you mind elucidating for one and all the general purpose of your visit?"

When the man failed to answer right away someone standing behind him called out, "He wants to know how come you're hassling him, Earl."

"Oh, yeah, that." The giant jerked his right thumb over his shoulder. "Floyd there tells me you guys don't care for our domestic beer. Is that so?"

"My friends might have expressed a desire for an import—" McCarter held up his empty can of Coke "—but if Coca-Cola Classic isn't domestic, I don't know what is."

The bruiser grumbled and flicked the empty can from McCarter's hand. "Coke don't count. I'm talking beer, mister, not a can of sugar water. Now, is it true what Floyd told me, or not?"

"Is Floyd the balding gentleman at the bar wearing the ridiculous lime-green vest and matching bow tie?" McCarter asked.

"The tie and the vest happen to be Floyd's trademark, mister."

"We all have our crosses to bear," McCarter said.

"Listen, smart ass." The big man leaned down so his face was an inch from McCarter's. His foul breath was a combination of garlic, fried onions and beer. "I don't know how they do things where you come from, but here at the Luva Brewski we don't take kindly to a bunch of high mucky-mucks marching in like they own the place.

"A bottle of import once in a while is fine, but mostly Floyd expects customers to drink domestic. And you know what, mister?" He squeezed his thumb and forefinger together. "Me and Floyd think just like that."

"My condolences to Floyd," McCarter offered, then added quickly, "I don't suppose this Buy American campaign of yours carries over to the domestic automobiles you manufacture?"

"As a matter of fact, yeah," the man stated. "Something wrong with that?"

"Not at all," McCarter said. He glanced around and leaned forward to continue in a stage whisper. "But I think you blokes ought to go outside and check the parking lot. I think I saw a Volkswagen out there."

"A Volkswagen?" The guy frowned.

"Maybe one of those damn Japanese cars, too," the Briton added. "You chaps better have some good sturdy rope so you can go out there and have a lynching party. Need a mighty strong rope to hang a car by its fender until it's dead."

"And may Detroit have mercy on its soul," James muttered as he finished off his beer.

"You kiddin'?" Earl said, not certain one way or the other.

"Heaven forbid," McCarter said with mock astonishment.

The bruiser blinked and ground his teeth as he moved back from the Briton. "Normally," he said, "spouting off to Earl Beaumont would land you in the hospital emergency room. I'll tell you what, mister. Never let it be said I took advantage of an out-of-towner too damn dumb to know when he's skating on thin ice. I'm going to let you off easy this time."

"We appreciate your consideration," Manning finally put in to defuse the tense situation. Too many of Beaumont's friends were itching for a fight. "There's no reason a difference of opinion has to lead automatically to violence."

"My feeling exactly," Beaumont agreed, then redirected his attention to McCarter. "So, the deal to let you off the hook is this, mister: you buy a round of domestic brew for me and all of my friends, and I let you walk out of the Luva Brewski in one piece."

"Fine," McCarter said without argument, digging into a pocket for a coin that he flipped onto the center of the table. "Here you go. Drink and enjoy."

"I said drinks for the house, smart ass." Beaumont picked up the coin and stared at it. "What the hell is this for?"

"The nearest pay toilet you can find," McCarter told him. "That way you and your mates can have all the drinks you want."

"There goes the party," Encizo advised James.

"No kidding," said James.

"And he actually had the nerve to ask me to trust him," Manning said.

Growling like a bear with a migraine, Beaumont charged, swinging both arms downward in a double-handed blow designed to make McCarter one with the tiles of the floor. But the Londoner had other plans.

Kicking back his chair and leaping to his feet, McCarter dodged out of the way as Beaumont's descending fists crashed on the table. The huge man's momentum carried him forward. While Beaumont fought to regain his balance, the fox-faced McCarter attacked, grabbed a handful of Beaumont's hair, forcing the bigger man's head to continue on course.

Beaumont's face connected with the schooner of beer and the schooner shattered. Beer splashed in all directions. Beaumont fell heavily on the table, which collapsed under the strain and deposited the over-sized autoworker on the floor.

Sitting in a semicircle around the wreckage of their table, Encizo, Manning and James searched the faces in the crowd to see what effect the fall of Earl Beaumont had on the rest of the bar's patrons. They had their answer when one of the men hefted a chair over his head and began sneaking up on McCarter.

"Down!" Manning hollered.

The East Ender heeded the Canadian's warning and ducked. The chair continued past him and slammed square into the back of the dazed Earl Beaumont, who had just staggered to his feet, knocking him to his knees.

The man who had thrown the chair kept coming at McCarter, but Manning got there first, stiff-arming the man in the chest, then bowling him over with a rock-solid punch to the chin. The stunned man sank in a heap to the floor.

"Cheers," McCarter called to Manning, then turned to confront another pair of brawlers looking for trouble. McCarter made sure they found it.

Meanwhile, Calvin James and Rafael Encizo had left their ringside seats to join the fight. Two Luva Brewski customers singled out the stocky Cuban and attacked in a flurry of swinging fists.

Encizo deftly sidestepped his first opponent, butting him across the back of his skull with his elbow as the man rushed by. The man grunted and slumped to the floor unconscious.

Having seen his friend succumb to the Cuban's swift defense, the next assailant was less anxious to confront Encizo man to man. He decided the only way to walk away a winner was to play dirty. The autoworker seized a chair and turned it so its legs were pointing out. "I'm going to stick you like a bug," he boasted.

"You're welcome to try," Encizo invited.

The man with the chair hunkered down his shoulders and charged, planning to nail Encizo in the back when the Cuban turned to flee. But Encizo did not budge. When the chair legs were almost touching him, he leaned back with his weight on his right foot and kicked out with his left.

His foot penetrated the flimsy wicker seat of the chair and plowed into the stomach of the man behind it. Air whooshed from the startled man's lungs. Encizo shook his foot free and flung the broken chair away. Then he swept in to polish off his adversary, changing his mind when the man he had kicked toppled to his hands and knees and began losing his lunch.

Metal glinted in the dim light of the bar as a man with a knife attacked Calvin James. The black Phoenix pro was not impressed. Growing up in Chicago, he had seen youths of ten with a finer fighting stance. The fool facing him now was an amateur.

Slashing back and forth as if carving a turkey, the overconfident knife-wielder suddenly changed tactics and stabbed the blade outward. James saw the move coming and shifted to the left as the knife flashed harmlessly by.

James caught the hand holding the knife and chopped down on the wrist with the edge of his other hand. The ulna bone broke with a dry snap. The fingers holding the knife opened and the blade fell to the floor, its owner clutching his injured wrist and scurrying away before James could inflict further damage.

Several more of Earl Beaumont's drinking buddies tried their luck at bringing down the four Phoenix Force soldiers. None succeeded. When it finally dawned on them that it might be a good idea to take their thirst and aggression elsewhere, the Luva Brewski's customers deserted the bar as if it were a sinking ship. After the stampede only Floyd the bartender, a dazed Earl Beaumont and Phoenix Force remained.

"I don't know about the rest of you," McCarter said, massaging the knuckles of his right hand, "but I'm ready to head out to the airport now."

Manning shook his head. "Why couldn't you have left five minutes ago?"

"What?" McCarter asked. "And miss the punch-up?"

"Hey!" the bartender hollered from behind the sanctuary of his bar. "What the hell's the big idea coming in here and tearing up the place? Who's going to pay for damages, that's what I want to know."

"Not to worry, guv," McCarter advised, stepping over to where Earl Beaumont was sitting in the middle of the floor, his head in his hands. "I think Mr.

Beaumont here will be more than happy to cover the cost of whatever he and his friends destroyed." McCarter nudged Beaumont with the toe of his shoe. "Isn't that right, Earl?"

Beaumont sighed and dejectedly nodded his block-ish head.

"See?" McCarter told the bartender. "Not to worry."

"Now can we go?" Manning asked.

"Sure," the cockney replied. "Why not?"

From the breast pocket of Gary Manning's coat came a distinct low-level beep. Manning reached into his pocket and removed the source of the noise—a small rectangle of red plastic that could have been mistaken for a deck of cards.

The simple-looking device was, in fact, a highly so-phisticated SFPL—satellite fixed-point locater—that enabled Stony Man headquarters to determine its lo-cation virtually anywhere on earth to within an area a quarter-mile square. Manning deactivated the SFPL's alarm by pressing a tiny button on the rear of the de-vice.

"So much for our vacation," he told his friends, then turned to the bartender. "Any objections if I use your phone, Floyd?"

Floyd wisely said it would be all right.

While McCarter, James and Encizo waited, Man-ning went to Floyd's office behind the bar to tele-phone Stony Man. In less than two minutes the brawny Canadian returned.

"That didn't take long," James said. "What's the good word?"

"Does Uncle Halbert needs us?" McCarter asked.

Manning nodded.

"What about Katz?" Encizo asked.

"We'll pick him up on the way."

**4**

Colonel Yakov Katzenelenbogen completed his tour of New York's famous Wickemann Museum and thanked the curator for the enjoyment he had derived from the hours he had spent examining the collection. The Wickemann's exclusive exhibit had included some of the finest examples of Middle Eastern artwork the Israeli had seen in years.

Katzenelenbogen buttoned his coat, adjusted his woolen scarf around his neck, then made his exit into the chill winter air. Wind whipped around him as he carefully descended the slippery stone stairway to the sidewalk in front of the museum.

It was bitterly cold, but Katz seemed not to mind. The cold offered an invigorating change from the artificial warmth inside the Wickemann. A lone street-lamp cast its glow in a circle of light at the bottom of the steps as the Israeli colonel halted and decided what to do next.

Darkness had fallen hours ago, and his hotel was more than eight blocks away. It was ages since he had enjoyed the luxury of an afternoon to himself, and he was reluctant to end it. With that thought in mind, he ignored a taxi that sped by the museum in quest of a fare, pulled his scarf more snugly around his neck and started to walk.

A middle-aged man with iron-gray hair, gentle blue eyes and a face that radiated patience and wisdom, Yakov Katzenelenbogen could easily have passed for a college professor. Few would have guessed his true profession. Few would have dreamed such an outwardly mild man could serve as the unit commander for the toughest team of antiterrorists ever assembled. Yet the fact that his right arm had been amputated at the elbow was a clue to the truth.

Katzenelenbogen's life had been inexorably linked to warfare, espionage and counterterrorism since he was a teenager in Europe battling alongside French Resistance fighters against Nazi tyranny. After the Second World War he worked underground against the British in Israel's struggle for independence. Many years with Mossad honed his skills to perfection.

The Six Day War had taken its toll on Katz, first through an injury that lost his right arm to the fury of that brief but telling conflict, but more tragically by claiming the life of his only son.

Katz approached a corner as a fierce wind gusted in his face and snowflakes began to fall. He blinked and felt his eyes brim with tears. He was six blocks from his hotel. There was little evening traffic, pedestrian or otherwise. Another empty taxi hurried by, but the Israeli let it go. He was enjoying his walk.

Even before the two men stepped out from the doorway of an abandoned stationery store and blocked his path, Katz's sixth-sense warning system alerted him to their presence. They were in their early twenties and wore blue jeans and leather jackets, and ankle-high boots that made them appear taller than they were. Their jackets were open to the elements. They appeared not to notice the cold.

"Hold it there, Pops," the first man said. "What's the hurry, anyway?"

Katz halted and told the duo honestly, "I don't think it would be a good idea for you gentlemen to detain me."

"Oh, you don't?" The second man snorted. "Hear that, Tommy? Ain't that a kick in the can? Pops, here, is trying to tell us our business. Of all the nerve."

The punk named Tommy took a single intimidating step forward. "We ain't busted anybody in close to a week, which means Leo and me are out of practice. Understand? Now, it so happens your hike tonight cuts straight through our turf. If you want to pass, then you got to pay." He turned to his friend. "What do you think, Leo? How much do you think Pops can afford to cough up?"

"I feel like having me a steak dinner with all the trimmings, Tommy," the second hood answered. "Better make it forty bucks apiece, plus another twenty for the tip."

"Sounds fair to me. You heard what Leo said, Pops. You owe us a hundred bucks. Pay up."

"Do you know what it's like in hell?" Katz asked.

The question caught the hood called Tommy off guard and made him angry. "What kind of asshole question is that? What do we care about hell for?"

"Because," Katz said evenly, "that's where I'm going to send you and Leo if you punks don't get out of my way."

Tommy laughed. "It's your funeral, Pops. You're toast." He signaled to his friend. "Take him!"

Together the two muggers attacked their prey in a twin-pronged assault they had used numerous times before. Only this time it was different. Instead of quivering in his shoes like all their other victims, their latest target showed signs of resisting and putting up a fight. Neither of the Israeli's assailants could believe it.

The novelty of running up against someone unafraid of their threats of violence lasted as long as it took Katz to stun one of his attackers with a blindingly swift left backhand across the face. The Israeli's opponent reeled from the unexpected blow, jerking his head to the right as blood spurted from his nose.

"You're dead," the second thug proclaimed, his right hand streaking for the butt of a gun protuding above the waistband of his jeans.

Katz saw the move and reacted instinctively. While he usually favored a three-pronged prosthesis, there were times when Katz preferred to attract less attention and wore an artificial hand in a pearl-gray glove.

The purpose of the prosthetic device was more than cosmetic, though, for amid its insulated wires and cables, the hollow index finger of the steel hand housed the barrel of a built-in pistol. Firing a single .22 Magnum cartridge, the weapon was detonated by a 9-volt battery that could be activated by a manipulation of muscles in the stump of Katz's arm.

Not all sharks swim in the sea, and on more than one occasion the Israeli's hand had proved the deciding factor in whether he walked away from a confrontation with an enemy. Such was the case when Leo Banks reached for the gun at his waist.

Katz did not hesitate. He raised the steel finger of his artificial hand and fired. Flame erupted from the tip of the weapon's gloved barrel as the .22 Magnum bullet found and buried itself deep in the center of Leo Bank's forehead. The impact of the close-range blast knocked the target off his feet to the sidewalk. The body convulsed in one massive spasm and was still.

Seeing his friend die before his eyes did wonders for Tommy Renato's sense of self-preservation. But before he made his getaway, he had to kill the old man who had burned poor Leo. He owed Leo that much.

Tommy always carried a handgun when he worked the streets of New York. Not to do so was pure idiocy, he believed. As Katz turned toward him and charged, Renato's fingers closed over the butt of his gun. He was too slow. Before Tommy could pull out his gun Katz slammed into him, and Tommy Renato found himself backpedaling full speed in the direction of the abandoned stationery store.

Desperately, Renato tried applying the brakes. It was useless. With Katz shoving him with all the strength he could muster, Renato hit the store window with a crash. The window warped and buckled under the impact and, with one final push from the determined Phoenix Force pro, Tommy Renato smashed through.

Glass shattered into knives of death that butchered the writhing Tommy Renato in seconds. One razor-sharp shard cut cleanly through the wrist of the hand holding the gun. Renato screamed, thrashing around on his back as if his nervous system was on fire. Then a piece of broken glass the size of an ax blade pierced the shrieking hood's neck, and Tommy Renato's problems were over.

Katz stepped away from the window as an automobile pulled to a halt at the curb. The Israeli turned to the vehicle as its front passenger door opened and a familiar figure emerged.

"How're you doing, mate?" inquired McCarter.

"Good enough," Katz responded, noting as he did that the rest of Phoenix Force was waiting in the car. "Nothing I couldn't handle."

McCarter solemnly surveyed the damage. "What was it? Robbery?"

"They thought so," Katz said.

**5**

There were no batteries in the smoke alarm, but the oversight was intentional. Equipping the alarm with batteries would have been an exercise in futility thanks to David McCarter's Player's cigarettes.

They were seated around the conference table at Stony Man headquarters, and Brognola had just described to Phoenix Force the details of the president's visit earlier in the day. Now, having heard what their boss had to say regarding the matter, the five-man antiterrorist team opened up with their questions.

"The four DEA dudes who got wasted," Calvin James began, "were simply picked up off the streets of Bangkok, worked over till it hurt, then transported to this Bang Kwang prison where they were summarily executed less than two hours later. Is that it?"

"In a nutshell," Brognola confirmed. "The four dead agents never had a chance."

"Who the hell would have under those circumstances?" Manning asked. "How about the remaining DEA operatives in Bangkok?"

"There are seventeen others," Brognola said, "and the whereabouts and safety of each has been accounted for. Naturally, though, the rest of the DEA agents in Thailand are maintaining extremely low profiles."

"Which will place any investigations they may currently be involved in on hold," Encizo stated.

"Exactly," Brognola agreed.

"Do we know if the slain men were working together on an individual case?" asked Katz.

"I looked into that shortly after I met with the president," Brognola answered. "I had the most recent reports filed by the agents transmitted here from Bangkok. If the four men were participating in a joint investigation at the time of their deaths, their reports give no indication of that fact. So we have to assume at this point at least, that no connection between their individual cases exists."

"So why bump them off?" McCarter said. "To pull off something like that somebody had to go through a lot of aggravation. Could it be a vendetta of some kind?"

"Revenge could be behind the killings," Brognola said. "But if so, the elaborate arrangements leading up to the agents' executions would have been unnecessary. It would have been much easier just to gun them down outside the prison."

"Unless those responsible for the murders wanted the four deaths to serve as a warning," Manning suggested.

"To the rest of the DEA?" Encizo asked.

Manning shrugged. "Who knows?" Then he said to Brognola, "Has the DEA recently made any substantial busts in the Golden Triangle?"

"Nothing to write home about," the Fed replied. "A little bit here, a little bit there. Small stuff, mostly. In terms of creating any permanent roadblock to the manufacture or transportation of illicit substances in Thailand, Burma and Laos, the DEA efforts can pretty much be measured in inches instead of miles. Given the enormity of what they're up against, however, it's incredible the DEA gains any ground at all. They're too few trying to accomplish too much with too little support where it counts."

"So what else is new?" James said. "If the Drug Enforcement Agency was expanded and given the authority and personnel it really needs to get the job done, then maybe some of our elected officials would have to cut back on their annual taxpayer-funded, fact-finding missions to the Caribbean whenever the mood strikes. Heaven help them if they ever had to actually pay for their own vacations like the rest of the population."

"If the DEA isn't shaking any bigger trees than usual," Encizo said, "then the deaths of the four special agents might not be related at all to current drug investigations in Thailand. Perhaps we're looking for a connection where none actually exists."

"Which brings us right back to where we started," Katz said with frustration. "Let's run with what Rafael mentioned for a minute, though. If it's true that working for the DEA has no bearing on why the four Americans were murdered, then we have to ask ourselves who would benefit most by getting Uncle Sam angry with the Thai government over such an incident.''

"With the popularity of coups in that neighborhood,'' McCarter concluded, "it could be anyone.''

"I think we're talking smoke screen here,'' James told the group. "Keep the right hand busy—in this instance the Thai government—so the left hand—some jokers standing on the sidelines—can do whatever the hell it is they have in mind without interference.''

"That's a theory I can support,'' Brognola said. "In any event, that's one of the things you'll be flying to Bangkok to find out. Before he left Stony Man today the president made it abundantly clear that he wants the wanton slaughter of DEA personnel in Thailand to go no farther. Phoenix Force is authorized to take whatever steps are necessary to ensure that no more DEA special agents lose their lives.''

"Will we be going in blind on this one, Hal?'' Katz wanted to know.

Brognola understood the reason for the Israeli's question. With four operatives already dead, it was reasonable to assume that the remaining DEA officers in Thailand were under observation by those responsible for the killings. If so, then by working with the DEA people in Thailand Phoenix Force would blow their cover as soon as they arrived in Bangkok.

On the other hand, investigating the incident on their own could waste valuable time that could cost more lives, something no one wanted to happen. All things considered, then, the positive results of Phoenix Force turning to the DEA in Thailand for assistance far outweighed the possible negative outcome of their not doing so.

"No," Brognola answered Katz, "you won't be going in blind. That's not to say the DEA will roll out the red carpet for you when you arrive in Bangkok, either. Your contact with the DEA will be limited to one of their special agents. Agent Fisher will be notified to expect you approximately two hours before you touch down at Don Muang International."

"Who's this Agent Fisher going to think we are?" Encizo asked.

"Special investigators sent by Washington to learn more about the executions," Brognola said.

"In other words," Manning concluded, "he's going to think we're CIA."

Brognola chomped on his cigar. "If Agent Fisher wants to make that assumption, that's his business. From this end he'll be ordered to assist you in your investigation in any capacity he can, no questions asked.

"Fisher will also arrange for Thai customs to look the other way when your baggage comes through. To save time, I took the liberty of having most of your gear packed up. You're welcome to look over your equipment to make sure I haven't missed anything."

"Fair enough," Katz said. "How soon do we leave?"

Brognola glanced at his watch. "Ten minutes. Sorry for the rush, but you have to get to Los Angeles in a hurry to catch a Korean Air Lines flight bound for Bangkok."

"You've told us that of the DEA people in Thailand, only Agent Fisher will know we're coming," Gary Manning said. "What about the Thai government? Will anyone there be expecting us?"

"Not if we can help it," Brognola said. "Since we don't know the identity of whoever is behind the killings, tipping our hand in advance to the Thai government might prove unhealthy for you guys." He indicated Encizo and James.

During the Phoenix Force mission in Vatican City, both Calvin James and Rafael Encizo had been subjected to torture by their enemies. James had paid for that encounter by losing part of the little finger on his left hand, and a white-hot coin had been dropped in Encizo's palm.

"After what you two went through in Italy," Brognola continued, "I want to avoid any unnecessary breaches in security that could lead to more of the same."

"Amen to that," James agreed.

"You said it," Encizo added as the men stood to leave. "Some things are not better the second time around."

6

The five conspirators had not journeyed to the city of Pattaya, commonly referred to as the Thai Riviera, to frolic on the popular resort's sandy beaches. Nor had they come to play a round or two of golf, to try their luck at waterskiing or scuba diving or to purchase companionship for the duration of their stay.

They were interested in none of these things. With millions of dollars in future revenue riding on the success of their proposed venture, they had traveled to Pattaya for one thing only: to conduct business safely in the last place their enemies would expect to find them. United by greed, the five were setting aside their personal differences to achieve something that was only possible if they joined forces.

"It is time," Colonel Manoon Roopkachorn announced. "To tarry longer when there is so much yet to do is to tempt those who would like to see our plans fall through. Let the meeting begin."

He led the way to a table in the center of the room, beneath a ceiling fan whose wooden blades turned lazily. The intricately carved brass base of the table supported a thick circular piece of glass that ensured that none of the five men took precedence in the seating arrangement. At a round table every man was king.

Manoon pulled back his chair and waited for the others before he sat. He asked if anyone minded if he smoked, and when no one objected he removed a gold cigarette case from his shirt. He took out a Lucky Strike, put the case away, then lit the cigarette with a matching gold lighter.

Manoon sighed with pleasure as he inhaled the smoke deep into his lungs. "I confess it is a disgusting habit," he said, exhaling, "but which of us is above a little private vice or two?" He inhaled once more and then addressed the group. "On behalf of my brother and myself, I now officially welcome you to Thailand."

Manoon's younger brother, former Wing Commander Manas Roopkachorn, sat on Manoon's right. The family resemblance was striking. Both were tall and muscular, with hard jawlines and eyes of piercing black. Each wore his hair cropped short in a military cut. Both gave the impression that they would deal ruthlessly with anyone who opposed them. Manoon was fifty-two. Manas was forty-seven.

"After all this time it is truly remarkable to be sitting down together," Manoon continued. "For too long now we have let mutual distrust stand in the way of progress."

"Which is not to say that mistrust was not justified and well earned," Burmese Communist Party leader Lo Hsing Han felt obliged to point out. "But I for one am willing to forgive and forget. The door that we would open cannot be unlocked by keeping alive old prejudices."

"My sentiments precisely," Manoon said. "Wasting our time in petty competition will never bring us the riches we shall derive from working together."

"Let us get on with it, then," an impatient General Ma said. The eldest of the group, the general was leader of the Chinese Irregular Forces, who were also known as the Kuomintang, or KMT. Since 1961 General Ma and his people had served as middlemen for opium deliveries to Thailand from Burma.

"We all agree, Manoon," General Ma went on, "that we would be farther along now if we had settled our differences years ago. But let us not belabor the obvious. Clearly if we did not feel the time was right for our partnership, none of us would be sitting at this table."

Manoon, who had his own ideas about General Ma's overblown opinion of himself, smiled warmly and bit his tongue to keep from saying something he would later regret.

"Believe me, General Ma," he said, smiling, "I am as eager as you to get our partnership under way. If I appear to move cautiously, it is because I want nothing to stand between us and our success."

General Ma, finding no room for argument in what Manoon said, could only nod. "Very well, Manoon, your words ring of the truth. Please continue."

"Thank you," Manoon replied, mentally cursing the old fool for being such a pompous ass. Manoon was no fortune teller, but once their plans were under way he could foresee the day when General Ma would suffer an unfortunate accident. For the moment the prospect of such a mishap stilled Manoon's sharp tongue.

"We all know, good friends," he proceeded, "of the vast riches to be made selling slow death to the fools who would hasten the inevitable. It is and always has been a seller's market as far as heroin is concerned.

"You, Lo Hsing Han, have grown wealthy supplying the opium from which the heroin is made."

"I am a businessman," the BCP leader stated. "Luckily, I supply a product that is, as you say, much in demand. Our bumper crop last year was one of the largest ever and, this year's crop might even top that."

"And yet, thanks to the meddling interference of the Burmese government," Manoon pointed out, "you will never know for certain the true size of that crop."

"Not *my* government," Lo Hsing Han corrected. "The Burmese Communist Party has never accepted its right to rule. Be that as it may, the rest of what you say is true. Those in power within Burma have outlawed the Communist party and have decided that cultivating the fruit of the poppy is no longer an honorable profession.

"The government crackdown has been costly. Not only have I lost many of my people through violence against them, but much fertile land lush with beautiful poppies has been seized, the crops destroyed. Without poppies we cannot produce opium. Without opium we have no heroin. And without heroin I am a salesman with nothing to sell. Though my followers are many, I curse the fact that we are not yet strong enough to overthrow our oppressors."

"Yours is a tale we should pay heed to," Manoon commented. "The unprepared find history has a nasty habit of repeating itself. We have no wish to see the reckless attitudes of the Burmese government adopted in Thailand. We acknowledge your contribution to the impressive opium yields of the past, and mourn the loss of this year's harvest.

"But know this, Lo Hsing Han: just as you and your people have been made outcasts in your own country, the doors into Thailand are open to you and your cause. By uniting with us, you have guaranteed that the day will come when the Communist party will rule Burma."

"My list of enemies is as long as my patience," said the BCP commander. "I will enjoy watching them die."

"We all will," Manoon vowed, then turned to General Ma and the Burmese man sitting next to him. "Every poppy that is not lanced in Burma reduces the quantity of heroin that may be sold at your end of the chain.''

"Which is why General Ma and I agreed to hold open the doors into Thailand for Lo Hsing Han and his supporters." Chang Chi-Fu finally spoke. "It is written that a man may never know thirst until the day his well runs dry. Perhaps it is so. I have no intention of finding out.

"What has happened in Burma could easily happen here unless we take the necessary steps to avert disaster. Lo Hsing Han's loss has tapped the water of our well, but not drained it. As long as we repair the damage quickly, we shall continue to drink and quench our thirst."

Chang Chi-Fu, or Khun Sa, as he was also known, was the undisputed reigning warlord of the Golden Triangle. A former commander of the Burmese militia, he controlled his profitable domain with the aid of a legion of fighters loyal to his leadership, the San United Army.

Chang's influence within the Golden Triangle began in 1975, when he escaped after six years in a Burmese prison. At the time of his escape Burma was engaged in the first of a series of antinarcotics campaigns directed primarily against the KMT refineries and stockpiles operated by General Ma.

Never one to pass up an opportunity, Chang took advantage of the Burmese government's war on the more prominent narcotics traffickers and he promptly established a name for himself in the opium trade. He fled to Thailand and within four years, with the aid of his private army of followers, he had secured for himself roughly two-thirds of the Golden Triangle's heroin production.

Less than pleased with the unwanted immigrant, the Royal Thai government repeatedly tried to curtail Chang's activities. Every attempt ended in failure, including one launched in conjunction with the U.S. Drug Enforcement Agency in which the equivalent of a $25,000 reward was offered for Chang's arrest.

Chang had retaliated by informing local bounty hunters that he would pay handsomely for the killing of Americans in northern Thailand. Soon afterward, the price tag the DEA had put on Chang's head was removed.

"Enough of the problems of the past," Chang said. "I say on to the business at hand. Tell us, Manoon, what is the word from Bangkok?"

"I have nothing but good news to report there," Manoon answered. "From our informants I have learned that the executions at Bang Kwang prison of the four American narcotics operatives have had exactly the effect we wanted. Naturally, the Americans are angry."

"Too bad for the Americans," Lo Hsing Han lamented sarcastically. "Who invited them to poke their fat Caucasian noses into our affairs anyhow? The four men we had killed simply happened to be in the wrong place for them at the right time for us. That's their own bad luck."

"We all know what hotheads Americans can be," General Ma reminded the group. "How has Washington reacted to the news of the deaths?"

"No cause for alarm there," Manoon told him. "The U.S. has registered a formal complaint with the Royal Thai government, demanding a full explanation of the incident."

"Which will get them nowhere." Manas Roopkachorn laughed. "The powers that be here in Thailand cannot tell what they do not know. Since the Americans have no other source of information, their quest for the facts is hopeless."

"And with nowhere to vent its anger," Manoon added, "the United States can only impotently shake its fist in frustration and eventually forget that the executions ever took place. By then our sleight of hand in the south will have distracted both the Royal Thai government and the Americans sufficiently to suit our needs."

"In a manner of speaking," Chang Chi-Fu said, "we owe the Burmese government a debt of gratitude. If they hadn't ousted Lo Hsing Han from Burma, then we probably would not have agreed to come to terms and consolidate our entire operation under one roof.

"Ours is a beautiful plan. Once it is operational, Thailand will be the world's largest single heroin manufacturing and distribution center. By the time our confused opponents guess what we are up to, it will be too late to stop us."

**7**

The passengers who had boarded Korean Air Lines flight 015 were not amused when their scheduled 10:40 p.m. departure from Los Angeles to Seoul was delayed for more than an hour.

"We are experiencing minor mechanical difficulties," claimed the jumbo jet's pilot over the intercom. "Please excuse any inconvenience this delay may cause."

When this message was repeated for the fourth time sixty minutes later, many passengers responded with annoyed groans of protest. Then at twelve minutes before midnight five male passengers came on board. As soon as the five men were seated in the first-class section of the aircraft the pilot announced that flight 015 was ready for takeoff.

"Hmmph!" a middle-aged woman called derisively across the aisle to where David McCarter and Calvin James were sitting. "So much for our mechanical difficulties. For the life of me I don't know why some people think they're so much better than the

"As if they could," Manas scoffed. "Let them try."

"We will be invincible," Chang Chi-Fu pronounced. "Lo Hsing Han has the men. General Ma with his KMT, and I with my SUA, have the know-how, and Manoon and Manas have the important Thai contacts we need. We have the strength, the intelligence and the political influence we require to succeed. In my humble opinion, good friends, we cannot fail."

rest of us. I advise you gentlemen to plan your itinerary next time a tad more carefully. Of all the nerve!''

McCarter, who had the window seat, was considering an appropriate reply when James intervened.

"Forget it," he told the Briton. "It's not worth it. She might be flying with us all the way to Bangkok, and we'd never hear the end of it."

McCarter took another look at the woman's glare and decided James was right.

"Sorry, luv." McCarter leaned across James's seat and apologized. "You have my word that me and my mates will be more considerate in the future."

"See that you are, young man," she said.

McCarter smiled politely and settled back into his seat, muttering softly, "Old cow."

"I heard that," Manning said from the seat behind McCarter's.

The flight to Bangkok was a long one. After drinks and dry-roasted peanuts were served, many passengers reclined their seats and went to sleep, while others donned headphones to view a film about a group of precocious children who spoke like adults and followed a pirate's map to buried treasure. Before one-third of the cinematic dud had played, most of its captive audience had switched to a ride on the shut-eye express.

Eight hours later after two full meals and a repeat showing of the movie, the KAL jumbo jet landed in Seoul for a two-and-a-half-hour layover.

"Did you ever stop to think how much time we spend in the air?" Gary Manning asked Katzenelenbogen when they were finally airborne again.

Katz, whose aversion to flying was on par with McCarter's to unwrinkled clothes, could only answer, "I prefer not to. Ask me again when we're back on the ground."

Flight attendants served an appetizer followed by a lunch of Korean cuisine. Aware of the rigorous mission that lay ahead, the men of Phoenix Force tried to relax. All but McCarter. Sensing, perhaps more keenly than the others, the full extent of what was waiting for them in Thailand, McCarter found it difficult to do much more on the last leg of their flight than sip Coca-Cola Classic and chain smoke Player's cigarettes.

Finally the passengers were instructed to fasten their seat belts for the final approach to Bangkok's Don Muang International Airport. Not long afterward they were on the ground.

Katz was the first of the Stony Man crew to be spotted by Ralph Fisher, the DEA special agent. Fisher approached the Israeli while Katz was waiting for his luggage.

"Mr. Gray?" Fisher asked, addressing Katz by his cover name. "I believe you were expecting me to meet you."

"I was if your name is Fisher," Katz said, extending his left hand for Fisher to shake. "Pleased to meet you."

Fisher shook hands with Katz, then glanced from side to side. "I was told there would be five of you."

"Are we being watched?" Katz asked.

Fisher shook his head. "Not that I know of. Still, under the circumstances, I can't really be sure, can I?"

"I don't imagine so," Katz said.

Fisher was a tall man in his early forties with light brown hair worn in a crew cut, and a face full of worry. He wore a dark blue leisure suit and a white silk shirt, which was open at the collar. His fingers toyed with the sleeves of his coat as he nervously cleared his throat.

"Well?" he repeated. "What about it? Are there five of you guys or not?"

"Yes, Mr. Fisher," Katz said, "the information you received is correct. There are five of us."

And before Katz could say more, Manning and Encizo joined them, immediately followed by James and McCarter. Using their cover names, introductions were made while the supplies Hal Brognola had packed for them began to appear. When everything they had brought with them from Stony Man was accounted for, they made their way to customs. Instead of having their luggage subjected to a search—as he did with the majority of the passengers of the KAL flight—a Thai customs official on duty nodded knowingly and cleared Phoenix Force through without incident.

"Lots of stuff," Fisher said, noting the amount of gear the men carried. "Looks like you've come prepared."

"Can't play with your toys if you leave them at home," James said.

Fisher led Phoenix Force through the passenger terminal to a parking lot outside. He opened the back of a late-model Land Rover for the men to stow their equipment, then unlocked the doors up front for everyone to climb in. With Fisher at the wheel the Land Rover was soon cutting through the snarl of late-afternoon traffic leading into Bangkok.

"It's usually a forty-five-minute ride to the city," Fisher said as they drove. "Less time if we're lucky, which I doubt. I only found out I was supposed to come get you guys about an hour ago, so all I had time to do was book you a couple of rooms at the Ambassador, then hotfoot it out to the airport."

"We appreciate your meeting us on such short notice," Katz said.

"What else could I do?" asked Fisher. "My orders came right from the top of the totem pole. And you know how that is. I had no other choice.

"Seriously, though, if you guys can get to the bottom of this weird shit of the past few days, then I'm more than happy to chauffeur you around town while you're here."

"What can you tell us about the deaths of your four associates?" Manning inquired.

"Only a little beyond the obvious," Fisher said. "Dick Warren and three other men I worked with got the living crap shot out of them in the execution room of Bang Kwang prison a few nights ago. How it happened? Why it happened? None of the rest of us know. Only thing for sure is that our co-workers are dead and the rest of us are all pretty shook up about it.

"Not that you can blame us. The way we see it is it could have been any of us taking the final blow at Bang Kwang. We think it's only a fluke that Warren and the others bought the big one that way and not us."

"What're your people actually *doing* about the deaths?" McCarter asked.

"You're British, huh?" Fisher said. "I knew the Company was into hiring free-lancers, but you're the first I've met. Well, as to your question, though— most guys I work with figure this isn't exactly the best time to schedule a picket line to protest what happened. You know?

"They've gone underground or undercover, whatever you want to call it. Until we know for sure just who the hell's knocking off DEA personnel, the whole lot of us don't see why we should act like nothing's wrong. Me included. Business as usual could be suicidal. Forget that!"

"Any guesses on who set up the executions?" Encizo asked.

"God, in this country it could be anybody," Fisher said. "Somebody that hates Americans or somebody out to embarrass the Royal Thai government. Maybe both. Either way you end up with dead DEA agents. That's cutting too close to home.

"You know, the international press might have forgotten last year's coup attempt, but the Thais sure haven't. The government here is still counting its losses, doesn't know who it can trust. And I'm beginning to understand how they feel. So, who killed our people? I don't know. The fact that it was DEA who got iced, though, could have something to do with why we're in Thailand busting our chops in the first place."

"You mean the heroin," James said.

"And the opium before that." Fisher nodded. "Can't have one without the other, and nobody does it better than the bunch we're up against here."

"Before your friends were killed there were twenty-one agents assigned to Bangkok," Manning commented. "That can't possibly be enough personnel to do the job right."

"Try telling that to the taxpayers back home," Fisher complained. "The Golden Triangle, with territory in Burma, Laos and Thailand, is a seventy-five-thousand square mile area. It'll produce close to six hundred tons of opium this year, and that opium will be refined into sixty tons of pure heroin. And you know where most of that shit's going to end up? Right on the streets where the cheap taxpayers live back home—which is how they really pay the price for not helping us out in the first place.''

''Maybe American taxpayers would feel better about pitching in if they were sure some buyer for the Defense Department wasn't out purchasing seven-hundred-dollar toilet seats,'' McCarter suggested.

Katz, who happened to agree with his British friend, added tactfully before Fisher could respond, ''But even with ten times as many agents the DEA would still be hard-pressed to bring the heroin pipeline in the Golden Triangle to a halt.''

''You're right,'' Fisher agreed. ''It's an absolutely impossible situation, and it's not going to improve until all the nations of the world come to their senses and realize narcotics abuse affects everyone, whether they use the stuff or not. Until that happens the best we can hope for is to slow the bastards down.''

''You've highlighted the obvious for us,'' Encizo said. ''What about the 'little bit beyond' information you mentioned?''

With a sigh Fisher passed a slow-moving vehicle, then answered the Cuban's question. ''It could be a coincidence, but I doubt it. I stopped believing in co-incidences a long while back. It just so happens that the arresting officers and the prison honchos at Bang Kwang who approved and supervised the DEA executions have since pulled a vanishing act. Can't find any of them.''

''That's not so dumb on their part,'' Manning decided. ''They had to know that sooner or later the finger of blame would point in their direction. They got out while the getting was good. Even if they weren't actually involved in setting up your DEA pals, guilt by association can be a strong motivating factor. Some of them could be on the run or hiding out simply because they're scared.''

''I'll believe that when they can prove they weren't part of the sting operation that got my friends killed,'' Fisher retorted. ''Which brings me to the only real clue that might be of use to you guys. In the last reports the slain agents filed, we came across an interesting piece of information: the night they were killed each of the four men had appointments to meet the same Thai informant, a man used by the DEA often in the past. Nothing out of the ordinary there. The whole scheme starts to sour, though, when you realize the meetings were scheduled in four different parts of Bangkok, all at roughly the same time.''

''That has to be it,'' Katz said. ''The informant suckered your friends into a string of phony meetings and they fell for the trap. The rest of the tale we know. Who is this informant? What's he do?''

''His name is Sutha Nakhon.'' Fisher spoke the name as if it were a piece of dirt in his mouth. ''When he's not feeding us tidbits of information about his connections in the underworld, or dealing drugs to some of the city's addicts, he's been known to pimp part-time at a nightclub in Bangkok's Potpong district.

"To a limited extent we've kept our eyes open for him since the executions, but it's been tough, and so far he's eluded us. We can't mount a full-scale search for him and still keep the low profile Washington has ordered us to maintain till we know exactly what's going on. In the meantime, Sutha Nakhon's out there running around as free as a bird."

"Hopefully we'll soon have the opportunity to clip his wings," said James.

"As soon as we've checked into our hotel," Katz added, "we'll make finding this Sutha Nakhon our number-one priority."

"Suppose we do find him?" Fisher asked. "Then what?"

"Then we see what the man has to say," James answered. "I know it sounds like a cliché, but we really do have ways of making him talk."

"Even if he doesn't want to?" Fisher asked.

"Especially if he doesn't want to," James said. "You help us find Sutha Nakhon. We'll take it from there."

Fisher grinned. "Sounds like a winning combination to me."

"And a real losing one for Sutha Nakhon," James added.

**8**

"One out of ten Thais lives in Bangkok," Agent Fisher told Phoenix Force. "The city's population is more than five million people. At any time of day, especially when you're trying to go from point A to point B, all five million of them seem to be on the road."

The downtown Bangkok traffic that Fisher plowed his Land Rover through clearly illustrated his point. Everywhere the men looked, an army of bicycles, taxis, jeeps, scooters, buses and *thuk-thuks*—three-wheeled motorized pickups—vied for the limited space on the streets. The exhaust fumes rising over the gasoline-driven vehicles combined to produce a murky haze.

Adding to the congestion were the Thai pedestrians, who bravely risked their lives by darting between moving vehicles to jaywalk across the street. The resulting stop-and-start progress grated on the nerves.

Posing as five businessmen in town to sample Bangkok's exotic nightlife, Phoenix Force checked into adjoining rooms at the Ambassador Hotel, which was located on Sukhumvit Road in the center of the city's commercial and entertainment districts. Choosing to wait until later to dine at one of the hotel's five gourmet restaurants, Phoenix Force elected instead to begin at once their search for Thai informant, narcotics dealer and occasional pimp, Sutha Nakhon.

Though it was early in the day for Sutha Nakhon to be making the rounds of the bars and clubs he was known to frequent, Phoenix Force and Agent Fisher investigated these locations first. Several Thais questioned informed them, for a price, that the informant had been seen the night before, but the bribes bought no additional information.

"So we take a trip to Sutha's office," Fisher said after they drew a blank at the last bar on their list. "If we're lucky we'll catch him right in the middle of a sale." He turned the Land Rover down a crowded street that ended at a parking lot adjacent to a canal.

*"Khlonas,"* Fisher explained as everyone left the vehicle and locked up. "It's the Thai word for canal."

"Eerie," said James. "What's this Sutha got, an underwater office?"

Fisher shook his head. "He operates out of a small lacquerware factory a little way down the canal. We can reach it by boat in less than half the time we'd spend in the Land Rover."

Fisher paid the parking attendant several dollars' worth of baht—Thailand's currency—in advance, then led the way to a dock at the water's edge, where Thai outboard motorboats were moored beside sleek streamlined speedboats.

A Chinese man who looked like a used-car salesman sat at the end of the dock reading a newspaper. When he saw the six men he tucked the paper under his arm and displayed prominent gold-capped teeth in a grin.

"Good afternoon, gentlemen," the proprietor of the boat rental agency greeted them. "And to what do I owe the pleasure of your visit to my humble business?"

"We want to rent a boat for about an hour," Fisher told him, pointing to a streamlined silver-colored craft. "We will pay a fair rate for the privilege. But try to cheat us and we'll go elsewhere to do business, and I'll personally spread the word that you are a shyster."

"You do me a great disservice, sir," the Chinese boat owner said with an air of innocence. "You obviously have me confused with some less reputable businesses I would be happy to name."

"Stop talking or we're walking," Fisher said. "I've heard it all before. How much?"

"For one hour? Six hundred baht?"

Fisher laughed. "We want to rent a boat, not buy one. We'll give you four hundred baht and not a satang more. Take it or leave it." Fisher turned away from the man and signaled to the others. "Come on.

I know a better rental agency not far from here where the boats don't look about ready to sink.''

"Wait!" the Chinese protested. "Now that I have had time to consider your generous offer, four hundred baht seems a reasonable amount, after all.''

"That's more like it," Fisher said. Then, remembering McCarter's comment about U.S. Defense Department expenditures, he told the cockney, "Pay the man.''

Minutes later they were on the canal, in the sleek motorboat they had chosen. Twenty-five feet long and as compactly designed as it was streamlined, it had plenty of room to spare. Each Stony Man squad member had stowed his black leather equipment bag, filled with an array of weapons. Fisher powered the boat and they were away.

After the noise and congestion of the city streets, traveling freely along the muddy waters of the canal was a welcome change. Most of the traffic on the canal that late in the afternoon consisted of Thai longnecked boats full of tourists, as well as small outboards bearing Thai merchants and their wares.

Along the banks commercial buildings stood side by side with *wats*, ornately decorated Thai temples, some with *chedi*, pointed spires at the top, others with *prang*, rounded spires. These gradually gave way to a series of Thai-style homes constructed of teak. Here and there orchards lined the banks of the canal.

"Venice of the East is what they used to call Bangkok," Fisher said over the engine noise. "The canals were everywhere in the old days."

"What happened?" Encizo asked. "Did they dry up?"

"Hardly!" Fisher smiled. "Bangkok's at sea level and prone to floods more often than not. No, what happened to the canals was that they were filled and turned into streets, hotel sites and the like. A shame, too. I understand from reading that up until the last century the waterways outnumbered the streets. Not like today."

Bored by the guidebook information Fisher was spouting, and eager to reach the end of their ride, McCarter interrupted, "How much farther?"

"Another minute," Fisher said as he reduced speed and steered the boat toward a dock. From the dock a ramp extended to the back door of a small factory.

Fisher killed the engine for the last few feet, and the boat drifted to the dock in silence. Then Manning jumped out, clearing the gap of murky water and landing on the dock. James tossed the Canadian a rope that was attached to the bow, and Manning pulled the boat in and secured the line to a curved hoop of iron embedded in the dock.

The winter sun was beginning to sink in the west as the rest of the men climbed out of the boat. Streaks of scarlet and orange raced across the sky. Clouds danced in the glow of oncoming sunset. A cool breeze replaced the afternoon's comfortable warmth.

"Where in the factory is Sutha's office?" Katz asked the DEA special agent.

"Upstairs at the back, overlooking the canal."

Manning listened for sounds of activity within the factory. "Doesn't sound like anybody's home."

Fisher led the way toward the rear entrance, motioning for the others to follow. "You know, Mr. Green," he said, referring to the Canadian's cover name, "I do believe you're right."

And Manning was. The lacquerware factory was totally deserted, including the second-floor office where their Thai suspect conducted his narcotics transactions with local suppliers and addicts. A light layer of dust coating a desk gave the impression that Sutha had not used the office for several days.

"Sorry, guys," Fisher apologized as they headed down the ramp again toward their rented boat. "Win some, lose some. I know we struck out, but hopefully we'll have better luck tonight."

"Hopefully we will," Katz said.

Manning undid the rope and jumped in. Fisher started the engine and turned the boat in a leisurely semicircle for the return trip. Shadows skipped over the surface of the water now like so many ghostly fingers. The eastern horizon was already going purple and dark.

"I can understand Sutha not being in his office," McCarter said, "but what about the people who would normally be working at the factory? Where were they?"

Fisher shrugged. "Who knows? Maybe somebody paid them to take the day off. After what happened at Ban Kwang prison the other night, anything is possible."

Looking over Fisher's shoulder McCarter's eyes widened. "I think you should open up the throttle about now," he recommended.

Fisher frowned. "How come?"

A bullet pierced the fiberglass to Fisher's right and McCarter reached for his gun.

"One guess, mate."

**9**

The sound of two approaching speedboats grew louder. Four Thai gunmen, brandishing weapons, rode in each, with a fifth man stationed at the steering arms of the boat's outboard engine.

A second bullet ripped a hole next to where the first had struck Phoenix Force's boat. McCarter aimed his Browning Hi-Power to the left of Fisher and fired. Even when he was skipping over the surface of the canal it was impossible for the U.K. sharpshooter to miss. His 9 mm automatic roared and he saw his target go down.

As the Hi-Power's payload crashed through the Thai gunman's chest he emitted a horrendous scream. He flung his assault rifle into the water and pressed his hands over his wound in a futile attempt to reverse the inevitable.

Then Agent Fisher whipped their boat around a bend in the canal and their pursuers were temporarily lost from view.

Rafael Encizo zipped open his black leather tote bag and removed his H&K MP-5 machine pistol. "Can we outrun them?" the Cuban asked.

"We can try," Fisher shouted. "Maybe we should head for shore."

"Forget it," McCarter countered, trading his Browning for the Ingram MAC-10 he took out of his bag. "They'd pick us off before we could leave our boat."

"Here they come!" Calvin James hollered, gripping the S&W M-76 SMG he had packed.

Fisher gunned their engine for all it was worth as the pair of enemy boats appeared around the bend. Almost immediately the three surviving gunmen in the lead started shooting. Enemy bullets pelted the water on each side of Phoenix Force. Crouching as low as he could safely manage, Fisher rocked the boat from side to side and swerved back and forth in unpredictable movements.

Anticipating Fisher's evasive maneuvers, Encizo braced himself and sent a stream of hot lead flying at their water-borne attackers. Instantly the Cuban's MP-5 eliminated one of the Thai pursuers, transforming the top of the doomed man's skull into an ugly spray of blood and gore.

Blinded by the unexpected shower of red muck across his face, the killer behind Encizo's target wiped his eyes clean with the back of his hand, the last act of his life. Encizo's H&K continued its sweep of death unabated, churning the front of the Thai thug's upper torso into sticky paste. The force generated by the multiple 9 mm impacts lifted the corpse from its seat and dumped it into the water.

The second speedboat now skimmed past the first in a bid to come abreast of the boat containing Phoenix Force. For less than a heartbeat, with boat number one directly in their line of fire, the four killers in the second vessel were unable to shoot without endangering the lives of their friends.

Calvin James and Gary Manning did not suffer from this handicap. Firing simultaneously, the American from Chicago and his Canadian counterpart made mincemeat of their foes.

Wielding the .357 Desert Eagle that had served him so well in previous battles, Manning blasted away just as the second enemy craft cleared the bow of the first. The Eagle's devastating .357 minirockets ripped apart one of the persistent Thai assassins in a hailstorm of agony that dissolved into oblivion faster than the dying man's brain could realize he was dead. His body toppled forward in a useless heap.

The killer Calvin James set the sights of his M-76 on did not fare any better. The S&W chattergun spoke in a flurry of angry sentences that left no room for rebuttal. One moment James's opponent was cruising down the canal trying to bag an American trophy; the next he was full of too many holes and searching for a place to die.

Had they been alone on the canal with their Thai attackers, Phoenix Force could have finished off their adversaries right then in a concentrated barrage of autofire. They were prevented from this by the untimely intervention of a long-tail boat full of tourists traveling up the canal in the opposite direction. Caught by surprise at the gunfight taking place on the canal, the driver of the tourist boat had no option but to steer his sleek craft straight through the middle of the armed conflagration.

Yakov Katzenelenbogen had been ready to unleash the full power of his Uzi when he glimpsed the approaching tourist boat from the corner of his eye. His finger relaxed on the subgun's trigger as he barked an order to cease fire. The boat filled with tourists slipped between Phoenix Force and their Thai opponents.

Sensing correctly that Phoenix Force would not willingly harm the tourists, the Thai killers began chopping away with their automatic weapons. The helpless tourists never knew what hit them. Butchered where they sat in a span of three violent seconds, their bullet-riddled bodies twitched and danced with jolts of electric pain as they died.

The driver of the long-tailed boat abandoned the steering arm and tried to save himself by diving into the water. But his efforts came too late and were far too slow. No sooner had he released his hold on the throttle than a volley of lead burst open his belly as if it were an overripe piece of fruit. He perished watching the bloody mess spurting from his gut.

With the tourists and their driver dead, Phoenix Force no longer had a reason to hold back. Sickened by the wanton slaughter of the innocent bystanders, Katz was the first of the Stony Man soldiers to put one of the killers on ice. As all three speedboats raced down the canal, the Israeli's Uzi went to work, hosing down the gunman riding point on the second enemy boat.

Silhouetted by the rays of the setting sun, Katz's target suddenly erupted into a splotchy picture of dark red death. Succumbing to the onslaught of the swarm of 9 mm Uzi slugs, the killer twisted awkwardly in his seat and lost control of his own submachine gun, which proved instantly fatal to the final pair of killers in the first speedboat.

The killers' bodies flopped to the floorboards as their boat veered sharpy to the right and slammed headlong into the concrete loading dock of a small Thai business. With a crash it disintegrated into a shower of splinters and sparks, the fuel tank on its outboard engine exploding moments afterward into a dazzling ball of flame.

Seeing the smoke from the wreckage, the last of the Thai gunmen gestured wildly for the driver of his motorboat to whip it around. The driver complied, cutting back on the throttle and slowing while reversing in a tight semicircle. With the Thai subgunner laying down a line of fire to cover their retreat, the driver hit the throttle hard as the boat came out of its turn.

McCarter signaled for Agent Fisher to do the same, but the DEA man was already going through the motions of the turn. As their boat banked to the right, Phoenix Force leaned left, their engine straining as once more Fisher sent them racing in the direction of the setting sun after their fleeing enemies.

The gap between the two boats closed rapidly as both sped past the spot where the tourists had died. Alerted by the repeated exchange of gunfire, curious onlookers hurried to the banks of the canal to watch the show. Many Thais cheered as the boats raced by.

They were almost to the bend in the canal when the driver of the enemy vessel decided his passenger wielding the SMG needed help. Steering with one hand, the driver pulled out a handgun with the other and turned in his seat to try to get a bead on one of the American devils chasing him. The old man with the hook for a hand would be the first to go, he thought, as his speedboat entered the bend. He aimed and fired.

Fisher hit the bend in a wide sweeping turn that took them close to the left bank. The Thai killers shifted to compensate for the DEA agent's abrupt maneuver just as McCarter and James raised their weapons.

Trapped in a cross fire from which there was no escape, the two Thai assassins ended their lives in savage pain. Both men threw down their guns as a score of bullets peppered their bodies. The driver lurched against the throttle and sent the boat in a dizzy uncontrollable spin.

The dead men splashed overboard, and the unattended motorboat set a collision course toward the muddy bank of the canal. Momentum drove the boat into the mud, where the propeller blades quickly clogged.

Only bubbles marked the spot where the last two Thai gunmen had gone to their watery graves. Agent Fisher set the throttle at idle and give the engine a well-deserved rest.

"Well done, Mr. Fisher," Katz said. "You handled the steering like a champ."

"I can't take all the credit," Fisher said, genuinely relieved. "It's amazing what you can do when someone's trying to shoot your ass off."

"They came out of nowhere," Manning said.

"Yeah," McCarter agreed. "They must have seen us at the lacquerware factory searching for Sutha Nakhon."

"And now they're all dead," Encizo added. "Before we had a chance to question any of them."

"Seeing how they killed those poor tourists almost makes me glad none of the bastards pulled through," James said. "Still, we're not completely in the dark, not with this Sutha character roaming around. Maybe we'll nab him tonight. Let's hope so, because until we latch on to him or something better comes along, all we have is this." And he pointed to the bubbles breaking on the surface of the water.

## 10

"Problems?" asked Lo Hsing Han once Colonel Manoon Roopkachorn completed his brief telephone conversation. "It must be something serious for your people in Bangkok to contact you here in Pattaya. Tell us, Manoon, what has happened in Bangkok that we should know about?"

Manoon debated whether or not to reveal the full extent of the information he had just received. Should he tell all or merely part of what he had learned? He did not fear Lo Hsing Han's reaction to the news, nor that of his brother, Manas, or of Chang Chi-Fu. All were strong enough to withstand a change in the current without resorting to panic.

No, the reason Manoon hesitated to completely answer Lo Hsing Han's question was sitting in a cushioned chair in the corner of the room by the balcony: General Ma.

The general, Manoon reflected, was too used to having things done precisely to his liking. Put simply, the old bear was spoiled. How, then, would he react to what Manoon knew? Would General Ma insist on

disbanding their little partnership until a later date, or
would he be smart enough to realize that the distur-
bance in Bangkok scarcely represented a threat to their
operation? Manoon could not say for sure, but he
knew it would come back to haunt him in the end if he
attempted to conceal anything from the aging KMT
commander. Better in the long run to keep everything
out in the open.

"It is my duty to inform you," Manoon began, inhaling deeply from the Lucky Strike he had clamped
in a corner of his mouth, "that a group of my supporters, approximately ten men, clashed earlier today
with at least one representative of the American DEA
and five of his friends."

"Oh?" Chang Chi-Fu did not seem overly disturbed. "And where in Bangkok did this confrontation take place?"

"On the Khlong Samsen," Manoon replied. "The
Americans were attacked shortly after they visited a
lacquerware factory that is under my control."

"I don't understand, then," General Ma said,
sighing and leaning forward so his palms were braced
upon his knees. "If ten of your men clashed with the
Americans on the canal, as Lo Hsing Han has already asked, what is the problem?"

"Apparently, General," Manoon explained slowly,
"none of my people survived the attack."

"What?" General Ma's hands flew from his knees
as he surged to his feet. "Dead? All of them?"

Manoon nodded. "It would appear so. Yes."

Manas, who understood as his brother did how easily General Ma could disrupt all their plans, said hopefully, "Surely the Americans must have had outside help to defeat such an obviously superior force?"

As much as he would have liked to lie, Manoon could only shake his head. "No. Those who witnessed the battle insist that the five Americans fought alone. Our people were defeated in spite of the fact that they outnumbered our foes."

General Ma raised his hands into the air and started to pace. "Well, that's it, then, isn't it? Here we are with our grand scheme to set up the largest heroin production operation in the world, and already the damned American dogs have sniffed out our plot. Perhaps we should take this as an omen to proceed more cautiously."

"Let us discuss this a moment before we elect to bring down the curtain on our program," Chang Chi-Fu said, much to the Roopkachorn brothers' relief. "The loss of a single battle on Bangkok's canals does not automatically mean that the entire war is lost."

"Ha!" General Ma snorted, tapping his finger to his nose. "I know a disaster when I smell one, and I tell you I smell one now." He turned to Manoon. "Answer me this: if the Americans aren't on to what we're up to, then how is it they happened to be snooping around this lacquerware factory of yours?"

"To answer your question requires no guile or creativity on my part, General Ma," Manoon said, careful to hide his frustration. General Ma was behaving true to form. To expect the idiot to start acting sensibly would have been asking too much of one who had worn the mantle of a fool for so many years. "The Americans obviously went to my factory in search of a man I employ called Sutha Nakhon."

General Ma placed his hands upon his hips. "So he works for you. Why should the American drug enforcement people be interested in him?"

"With my blessing and encouragement," Manoon answered, "Sutha established a relationship with the DEA agents in Bangkok, selling the Americans information designed to disrupt the dealings of certain business competitors of mine."

"But if your Sutha was on such good terms with the Americans," General Ma interrupted, "then why would they send out five armed men to find him? And why now of all times?"

"I was coming to that," Manoon snapped with irritation. "May I be allowed to continue?"

"By all means." General Ma ignored Manoon's poorly concealed display of phony politeness. "I am most anxious to hear your explanation."

"Thank you," Manoon said. "When Sutha sold information to the DEA he did not always interact with the same agent. One day he might sell information to one, the next, to another. That way he was always assured of having access. Not even having one of his contacts transferred back to the United States could disrupt this arrangement.

"You are of course aware, General Ma, of the four DEA agents we had executed at Bang Kwang prison. What you are not aware of is that, on the night they met their deaths, each of the Americans had scheduled a meeting with Sutha Nakhon. Naturally, the meetings never took place."

"So that's it," General Ma stated as if he were speaking to a child of six. One day in the near future he would have the pleasure of disposing of Manoon, as well as Manas. The Thai brothers, especially the loudmouth Manoon, were too much of a nuisance. "The Americans were looking for Sutha today because they have recognized his role in luring the DEA agents to their doom. Certainly it must be apparent even to you, Manoon, that the knowledge Sutha possesses puts our entire operation in jeopardy."

"Without Sutha Nakhon the four agents who were executed would still be alive," Manoon objected. "We owe Sutha a debt of gratitude."

"Which I will be pleased to pay at his funeral," General Ma insisted. "Sutha's contribution to our cause might be immeasurable, but now that the Americans are searching for him he has become a liability. Sooner or later they will catch up to him. You know it as well as I."

"So what are you suggesting?" Manoon demanded. "That I order Sutha killed? Is that what you're telling me to do?"

"Any of us is expendable," General Ma told the Thai colonel, "if it means preserving the good of the whole. Yes, I am saying that it will be better for us all if your people in Bangkok find Sutha Nakhon before the Americans do.''

Manoon stubbed out his cigarette in an ashtray and immediately lit another. "And Chang Chi-Fu, and Lo Hsing Han, what of you? Do you agree with General Ma?''

"General Ma's proposal does have its merits," the former Burmese militia commander, Chang Chi-Fu, confessed. "I think I speak for Lo Hsing Han, too, when I say that I would sacrifice the life of one individual, no matter how loyal to our cause, if it preserved the safety of our alliance.''

Manoon glanced at Lo Hsing Han and saw at once that the Burmese Communist Party leader did, indeed, agree with Chang.

"The fact that the Americans failed to locate Sutha Nakhon today works in our favor, Manoon," Chang went on. "It means we stand a chance of finding him first. It's as simple as that. What he knows makes Sutha a dangerous man.''

"And as for the Americans," Lo Hsing Han thoughtfully added, "they, too, are dangerous. Ten of your dead followers prove that, Manoon, if nothing else. Perhaps it would also be best if steps were taken to eliminate them.''

"Tell me," Chang questioned Manoon, "did any of the witnesses to the battle on the canal provide a description of the Americans involved?''

"One was known to be a DEA special agent, a man named Fisher," Manoon replied. "The others have never been seen before. They included an older man with a hook where his right hand should be, and a black man. No descriptions of the remaining men were given."

Chang shrugged indifferently. "No matter. As long as your people know what this Agent Fisher looks like, then that is all we need. Keep an eye out for Fisher and the five Americans will not be far behind...not if they are all hunting for Sutha. The fact that they will be traveling together while they conduct their search will only make the task of finding and killing them that much easier."

General Ma muttered as he returned to his cushioned chair and sat. "If Manoon's witnesses reported that this Agent Fisher's friends were new to their eyes, then it probably indicates that the American DEA has called in reinforcements."

"Or else the CIA," Manas reluctantly proposed.

"No matter," Chang repeated. "While the Americans are looking for Sutha, Manoon's people can be looking for them. And when they are found..."

"The *farangs* will die," Manoon promised.

"Yes," Chang said, smiling. "The foreigners will die."

**11**

"What's this?" McCarter asked.

"A raisin," James said.

"You're daft," McCarter insisted. "Since when do raisins have legs?"

Manning put down his fork and pushed his plate away. "That about does it for my appetite, thank you."

"Well, I think it's delicious," Encizo said, spooning another dollop of sauce over his rice, "whatever the hell it is we've been eating."

"There are times," Katz advised, "when it's best not to know."

Agent Fisher attacked his dinner with reckless abandon. "When it comes to dining in Thailand, if it can crawl, swim, fly or run, the Thais have a recipe for it. Not all local dishes are suitable for less adventurous Western tastes, mind you, but by and large Thai cooking represents some of the finest cuisine in the world."

Deferring to the agent's greater experience when it came to Thai food, Phoenix Force had given Fisher the green light to make selections on their behalf from the Ambassador Hotel's Thai restaurant menu. Fisher had accepted the challenge with relish and had ordered a dazzling array of culinary delicacies that not only tickled the palate, but at times threatened to burn a hole through it, too. Only Encizo, working his knife and fork over his plate in a constant blur of motion, seemed immune to the more volatile of the items.

Their meal had begun with appetizers of cashew nuts, deep-fried shrimp and crispy noodles, and continued with a bowl of steaming hot *tom yaam gung*, a lemon shrimp soup seasoned with makrud leaf. Next came the main dishes—sticky rice, chicken curry sweetened with coconut milk, ginger beef and fried chicken with mint and cloves. Sauces provided included sweet plum, dark soy and a fish sauce that the Thais used as a salt substitute.

A fourth sauce was also served, but it was only after McCarter had consumed half of it with his rice that Fisher confessed its origin—winged beetles, caught during the night and then crushed and mixed into the spicy concoction McCarter had been relishing.

Upon learning the truth the cockney gulped. "Beetles?"

"Yeah, yeah, yeah," Fisher sang softly.

"Cheers, mate," McCarter said. "That's one I owe you."

"I wouldn't hear of it," Fisher protested. "My pleasure."

The next course was a dessert called *salim*, consisting of sweet noodles in coconut milk, topped with small ice cubes and coconut meat. Even McCarter agreed that *salim* was a delicious conclusion to an unforgettable meal.

"Very good, then," Fisher announced once everyone had finished eating. "Now that dinner is behind us, what do you say we try and find Sutha Nakhon?"

McCarter replied as he held up a can of Coke, "I'll drink to that."

IT WAS SATURDAY NIGHT and the Potpong area of Bangkok, on a privately owned street between Silom and Surawong roads, looked nothing at all like the district Phoenix Force had visited earlier in the day. Transformed by darkness into a neon jungle of lights, Potpong was an unbroken line of movie theaters, massage parlors, restaurants, rent-by-the-hour hotels, nightclubs and bars.

After maneuvering the Land Rover through a tide of taxis, *thuk-thuks* and pedestrians, Agent Fisher finally managed to find a parking space. Everyone climbed out and the DEA man locked up.

"While it's true Potpong is popular with the locals," Fisher said as they began to walk, "the district caters mainly to a European clientele. The place has a reputation for being hot, and I'm talking vice with a capital *V*. Anything and everything is for sale here. Bangkok has more than three hundred thousand prostitutes, and Potpong is where most of them quite

literally let it all hang out." He halted to light a cigarette, then turned to Katz. "How do you want to work
this?"

"You're the one who knows what Sutha looks like,"
the Israeli commando answered. "We'll stick with
you, starting at one end of the street and working our
way down."

Fisher nodded. "Fine. If Sutha's out pimping tonight, then we'll find him. He's not exactly Mr. Low
Profile when it comes to doing business. He's a flashy
son of a bitch with plenty of money, and he enjoys
letting people know it."

For the next ninety minutes Fisher led Phoenix
Force from one Potpong nightspot to another.
Hawkers outside each establishment loudly invited
passersby to fulfill their wildest fantasies inside. Those
accepting that invitation found no surprises; the
nightclubs reeked of alcohol, thick smoke and scan-
tily clad women whose costumes left nothing to the
imagination and who gyrated to the beat of songs that
should have died with disco.

The massage parlors were even more depressing.
Behind windows of one-way glass women were displayed like cattle on an auction block, numbers attached to their skimpy uniforms serving to identify
them to potential customers. The fishbowl approach
to sex on the hoof was hard to take.

"As you might have guessed," Fisher informed
them as they left behind a particularly seedy massage
parlor, "not all of the girls working in Potpong are

here by choice. A large percentage of them are, in fact, indentured servants.''

"And all that shit boils down to is a fancy name for slaves," James said with disgust.

"It'll take us at least another hour to finish checking all the establishments in Potpong where Sutha Nakhon might be," Fisher said as they made their way to the next stop, a club called the Bottom Line. "What are your plans if we get to the end and still haven't found him?"

"That's easy," Katz answered. "We start over at the beginning."

The Bottom Line was yet another example of Potpong's cookie-cutter approach to late-night entertainment. Ignoring the energetic shill manning the entrance, Phoenix Force and their DEA guide went inside.

Immediately, a tide of noise washed over them courtesy of a six-piece Filipino house band whose one purpose in life seemed to be to prove that rock and roll had never died, just moved to Manila to be exported. The chubby lead singer sported a black leather jacket and sang in an emotive style that was rich in hair oil and feedback.

The club was packed with a raucous throng, many of whom were escorting beautiful Thai hostesses. As Fisher had explained, a majority of the men appeared to be Europeans out for a night on the town, searching for a good time. Bars at opposite ends of the club were doing their best to aid them in their quest.

Smoke in the dimly lit Bottom Line rose to the ceiling to form a thick gray haze. Mirrors lined the walls. A mob of bouncing bodies clumped in front of the bandstand indicated that the place had a dance floor. In addition, young Thai women danced topless on a dozen raised platforms situated beneath spotlights throughout the club. Like their sisters working elsewhere in the district, they identified their availability for extracurricular activities by the numbers attached to their tiny bikini bottoms.

Fisher led the men of Phoenix Force farther into the crowded interior of the nightclub, stopping every few feet to glance from side to side. Then suddenly the DEA special agent came to a halt.

"Paydirt," Fisher said over the din of the Filipino be-bop. "There he is. Third guy from the end of the bar on our left."

Sutha Nakhon would have been hard to miss. Decked out in baggy white trousers and a flaming red silk shirt, the man they had spent the day looking for also wore enough gold to open his own jewelry store. He was haggling with an overweight man wearing a cowboy hat and pointing at a woman who danced topless on a nearby platform. He seemed to be all smiles and persuasion.

"I just love it when a man enjoys his work," Manning commented. "How about cutting short his business transaction and inviting him outside for a chat?"

"I'll handle it," Fisher said, starting forward. "Sutha will recognize me. If you try to get him outside he might panic and make a scene."

"Be my guest," Manning offered. "All I want is a chance to talk to the guy."

Fisher began working his way through the crowd surrounding the bar toward Sutha. He was still more than fifteen feet away from his goal when Sutha happened to look to his left and see the DEA operative. The informant's expression told all as his eyes opened wide and his smile evaporated in a gasp of shock.

Fisher caught Sutha's reaction and immediately began shoving people out of the way to get at him, but by then the wily pimp and narcotics dealer was looking to break the world's record for the hundred-yard dash. Thinking the man chasing Sutha intended to stand between him and a romp with the topless dancer, the beer gut wearing a cowboy hat whom Sutha had been talking to reached out to stop Fisher. Fisher easily sidestepped the clumsy move and decked the cowboy with a sharp right-cross to the jaw.

Phoenix Force fanned out as Sutha wormed his way through the crowd, and the desperate Thai informer realized for the first time that Fisher had not come to the Bottom Line alone. This seemed only to redouble the fleeing man's efforts to escape. Ducking low and running at a crouch, he dropped out of sight amid the traffic jamming the dance floor.

"Where is he?" James shouted to Encizo.

The Cuban swore. "Damned if I know."

Katz and McCarter scanned the sea of faces on either side of the bandstand, searching for their quarry. So did Gary Manning, but from a location nearer the Bottom Line's second bar. Then Bobby and the Baluts finished their set and the people laying siege to the dance floor began to disperse, once again exposing Sutha Nakhon to his pursuers.

Encizo spotted the elusive informer first and rushed to bring him down. Sutha jumped when he saw the stocky Cuban coming at him and threw the first thing at Encizo he could grab—one of the topless dancers as she climbed down from her platform.

The startled woman shrieked as she was thrown into Encizo's arms, but she quickly calmed down when she realized he was not going to harm her. He disentangled himself from the unexpected embrace as Sutha darted away.

Alerted by the dancer's cry of alarm the rest of Phoenix Force and Agent Fisher watched Sutha leap up on a chair and across a table, running as fast as he could for the front door of the club. Only Manning was close enough to try to stop the Thai pimp's hasty exit. As Sutha flew past Manning the Canadian's right hand flashed out, his fingers brushing against Sutha's shirt.

Manning closed his fingers around the silk just as Sutha threw his weight forward. With a ripping sound Sutha broke free, leaving the frustrated Manning holding a long jagged strip of the red fabric.

Sutha reached the front door. He butted it hard with his shoulder, opening it with a crash and giving himself a taste of the freedom he wanted.

"Not if I can help it," Manning muttered to himself, throwing away the remnants of Sutha's shirt and charging out the front door after the man.

Katz and the others were not far behind, but by the time they hit the sidewalk, Manning was vanishing around a corner at the far end of the street.

"How fast is your friend?" Fisher asked Katz.

"Fast enough," Katz said honestly. "He should be able to catch Sutha, all right."

"Yeah," Fisher said. "But if he doesn't, then we're right back where we started from, which is nowhere."

McCarter pointed to an alley at the side of the nightclub. "Where does that lead?"

"To the next street over," Fisher answered. "In the same general direction Sutha and your friend are running."

"Come on, mate," McCarter said, tapping Encizo on the shoulder. "Let's see if we can head Sutha off at the pass."

"You got it," Encizo said, as he and McCarter rushed off down the alley.

"And we can go this way." Fisher began leading Katz and James in the opposite direction. "We'll circle the block and corner Sutha if he somehow manages to get that far. Can you handle that okay?" he said to Katz.

But the Israeli was already setting the pace for the run. "Try to keep up with me."

ENCIZO AND MCCARTER were midway down the alley when four women suddenly barred their way. Illuminated as they were by a light hanging from a wire stretched across the alley, their appearance—long skirts slit to their thighs, tight-fitting blouses over well-endowed chests and enough eye makeup to camouflage a tank—left little doubt in the Cuban's or Londoner's mind as to how the women managed to make ends meet.

Encizo slowed as he swerved left to dodge the women, while McCarter jogged to the right.

"Not tonight, ducks," McCarter said with a wink. "Me and my chum have a previous engagement."

Without warning the two women nearest McCarter and Encizo lashed out with a couple of perfectly timed roundhouse kicks that caught each of the Phoenix pros in the abdomen. Air whooshed from their lungs, and the duo doubled over in pain. Before they could recover, the first two women whirled out of the way to give the second pair a chance to work.

"Bloody hell!" McCarter yelled as he was kicked against the side of a wall. "Bugger all!"

One of the women snarled and charged the cockney in a style the British ace recognized as that of Thai kick-boxing. McCarter instantly took an on-guard stance, meeting his opponent's attack as her foot flew toward his chest.

McCarter blocked the kick with his left arm, then caught the kicking foot before it had time to withdraw. Wrenching the limb sharply with all his strength in a counterclockwise twist, he heard the tarsal bones in the foot snap with a satisfying crack. McCarter released the foot and his opponent collapsed to the floor of the alley with howls of agony that sounded too husky and deep to be feminine. The Briton promptly added insult to injury by planting the toe of his boot squarely between the howling figure's legs, producing an even more frantic exhibition of pain.

Encizo, who was having his own difficulty keeping one of their enemies' vicious kicks from landing, called out to McCarter, "That's no way to treat a lady."

"This ain't no lady," McCarter confessed, kicking his opponent a final time for good measure. "This one has balls!"

Encizo deflected a kick aimed at his head and retaliated handily with one of his own, catching his attacker in the same place as McCarter had, and immediately eliciting similar results.

"Hey, Mac!" Encizo turned to defend himself. "Mine's no lady, either."

Nor were any of the Thai "women" what they seemed. Their feminine appearance notwithstanding, the four who had challenged McCarter and Encizo were *kra-toeys*, Thai transvestites. That didn't alter the fact that the two remaining Thais the Phoenix pair faced could prove lethally dangerous.

McCarter and Encizo had other ideas.

Encizo dropped below a roundhouse kick that sailed harmlessly over his head, then countered when the *kra-toey* he was facing lost his balance. Attacking with a jumping knee and elbow strike, he slammed into the Thai's back, smashing him in the kidneys. The guy groaned and sank unconscious to the alley floor.

Only one of the original four attackers was still on his feet, but if he was disturbed that all his friends had been dispatched, the Thai transvestite did not show it.

Just then a burst of gunfire came from the direction of the Bottom Line, telling McCarter that Katz and the others were in trouble.

The *kra-toey* momentarily diverted his attention to the shooting, and that lapse of concentration was all McCarter needed. He stepped forward and chopped the man across the throat before he knew what hit him. The Thai gurgled and spit blood as he fell to his knees and died.

McCarter pulled out his Browning Hi-Power and chased after Encizo, who was already running back up the alley to help their friends.

## 12

Katz, James and Agent Fisher were nearing the corner they intended to round when a three-wheeled *thuk-thuk* rumbled off Silom Road onto Potpong, swerving in and out of traffic, directly toward the men of Phoenix Force and their DEA escort.

Two Thais rode in the cab of the motorized pickup, with five passengers in back. The weapons brandished openly left no question of their purpose.

Then a second *thuk-thuk* came speeding off Surawong Road from the opposite direction, it, too, carrying an armed crew of grim-faced Thais with one thing on their minds.

"How many calories in a lead sandwich?" James asked, drawing his Colt Commander from shoulder leather.

"Too many," Katz answered, taking out his SIG-Sauer P-226. "But who's counting?"

Amazed that Katz and James were so calm in the face of overwhelming danger, Agent Fisher withdrew his government-issue Beretta 92SB-F just as one of the

Thais in the farther vehicle lifted his automatic rifle to get things rolling.

Calvin James got there first, squeezing off a pair of .45 blasters from his Colt at the fatally slow rifleman. The bullets hit the man in the chest, flipping his body from the back of the Thai pickup and onto the hood of a parked car.

The dead man was tumbling to the street when Katz unleashed a triple salvo of bad news through the windshield of the nearer *thuk-thuk*. The two men seated in the cab died instantly, the driver wearing a bloodshot third eye in the centre of his forehead, his passenger slipping through the door with a bullet-shattered heart.

Driverless, the Thai vehicle hopped a curb and came to a crunching halt against the double-door entrance to another of Potpong's glittering nightspots. The three-wheeler's sudden stop threw the four assassins in back off balance. Katz attempted to bring one of them down but only winged the man in the shoulder before the second group of Thai hit men got into the act.

With pedestrians screaming and fleeing for their lives, the gunmen in the *thuk-thuk* approaching from the right began shooting even before the driver stopped the minipickup. The multiple gun blasts reverberated like a string of cheap firecrackers.

Katz, James and Fisher dived behind a parked car just a heartbeat ahead of the lead hailstones the Thais were tossing at them. Window glass shattered on the car. The sideview mirror on the passenger side was blown off, landing in the gutter.

A fresh volley of bullets from the left blew out the taillights. The Thai killers who had survived the crash of the first *thuk-thuk* were moving in.

Katz looked over his shoulder. The unbroken wall of a Potpong nightclub stared back at him. The entrance to the place was more than thirty feet away on his left, no help as an avenue of escape. Less than fifteen feet to his right, a door led into a massage parlor, but, again, it might as well have been on the surface of the moon. Trying to reach either door was suicide.

But the Phoenix team leader knew that the automobile they were using for cover would not hold out forever. At the rate the enemy was peppering the car, it, too, would soon become an invitation to a funeral.

Katz looked beneath the car. A pair of legs in cotton trousers were sneaking up from the left. He leaned on his shoulder and aimed at the legs with the SIG-Sauer P-226, firing when he was certain of a hit.

A 9 mm parabellum round shattered the advancing assassin's kneecap and sent the wounded man into a moaning slide to the pavement. Writhing, the Thai killer still managed to point his weapon at the Israeli colonel.

Some people never learn, Katz thought as he triggered his pistol again.

The Phoenix Force commander hit the gunman with two more 9 mm messages of destruction. One bullet drilled through the man's throat, tearing to pieces his carotid artery and thyroid cartilage. The other slug pierced the bridge of his nose and tunneled into his brain. The man fell, dead.

"Well," James muttered to Katz, "we sure pushed somebody's button and got a reaction."

"You noticed that too, eh?" Katz remarked, glancing around to make sure no one tried to creep up on them.

"You got something on your mind, Fisher?" James asked, noticing the DEA special agent was shaking his head with dismay.

"I was just thinking I'm glad to be alive," Fisher replied with a weary-sounding sigh. "At least until the bastards rush us, I am."

"LET'S RUSH THEM," Kitti Daungprateep urged in between shots. "If we all charge at once, the stupid Americans won't stand a chance."

"Don't be so sure of that," warned the man next to Kitti, pointing with the smoking barrel of his gun. "I'm sure Suwat thought the same thing, and look what happened to him when he got too close to those devils. First they shot him in the knee, and then they killed him."

Kitti took another couple of shots, then said, "That's because Suwat didn't have a plan. Suwat was always leaping first and looking later. So now he's dead. He should have had my plan."

"Which is?" the man beside Kitti asked.

"Let's rush them," Kitti said. "They won't know what hit them if we all attack at once."

In the end all the Thai gunman could get from his companions was their assurance that they would provide all the cover fire necessary for Kitti to storm the enemy's position on his own. Fair enough, he thought, branding each and every one of his so-called friends a coward and a fool. He would rush the Americans by himself, would surprise the Americans by himself and kill them by himself. And after the deed was done and Colonel Manoon Roopkachorn found out what had happened, the name of Kitti Duangprateep would be spoken of with the respect reserved for fighting men cut from the same tough bolt of cloth.

"Cover me, then," Kitti said, dashing from the *thuk-thuk* parked in the middle of the Potpong Road while his cohorts complied with their promise to protect him. A short distance to go and the lives of the puny Americans would be his for the taking.

"SOME CLOWN COMING IN at two o'clock," James announced, watching from underneath their cover car as a Thai from the second *thuk-thuk* charged in their direction. "What does he think we're doing back here? Sleeping?"

"I've got him," Fisher said, inching forward and slowly bringing his 92SB-F around the front bumper. He aimed at the rapidly advancing figure and fired twice, both the Beretta's 9 mm slugs dusting the charging Thai killer off his feet and into his grave.

When they saw Kitti cut down, his associates lost their reluctance to rush the Americans.

"Kill them!" screamed an enraged Chavarit Booncharoen. "So that Suwat and Kitti and all the others will not have died in vain, kill them all!"

And with the cry of a warrior with superior numbers backing him up, the Thai assassin charged, joined immediately by the five killers from the second minipickup. Each Thai triggered his weapon as he ran. Taking the rush as their cue to come out of the woodwork, the three holdovers from the wrecked *thuk-thuk* charged also.

Bracing themselves for the attack, Katz, James and Fisher were preparing for a final confrontation with their opponents when a fresh outburst of gunfire, to their right and farther up the street, reached their ears.

"And about time, too," James said.

Fisher was in the dark. "Huh?"

"The cavalry to the rescue," James said.

Having safely led his followers almost all the way to where their American victims were waiting to die, Chavarit Booncharoen was speechless when Rafael Encizo and David McCarter came rushing out from the alley alongside the Bottom Line nightclub, their handguns blazing a trail of doom and destruction as they ran.

Chavarit blinked in shock at the sight of the two newcomers running boldly out into the open as though completely unafraid. Such disregard of danger was nothing short of madness.

And the madness was catching. Alerted by the sounds of Encizo and McCarter in action, Katz, James and Fisher left the scant protection of the car and picked up the new set of rules McCarter and Encizo had brought to the game.

The enemy Thais began falling as quickly as the cockney and his Cuban counterpart started shooting. A dumbstruck Chavarit Booncharoen fell first, courtesy of the brief ride McCarter gave him on the Hi-Power express. Encizo's aim was equally deadly, a sobering fact two more assassins discovered just before the bullets from his Walther PPK put them permanently out of commission with a pair of .380-caliber headaches.

Trapped inside a cross fire from which no escape was possible, three more hit men paid with their lives for grossly underestimating the strength of their opponents.

Katz caught one of the gunmen with a body-ripping shot that unmanned him in a searing flash of agony. The instant soprano sang a few high notes in praise of death, then bowed out.

Another of the attacking Thais was the target for a pair of lead relatives from McCarter's Browning. The 9 mm duo burned a trail between the loser's rib cage and smashed the hapless man's heart and lungs. The killer tossed away the submachine gun he was wielding, and clamping his fingers over his twin entry wounds, spilled to the street in a lifeless heap.

James and Fisher played the execution waltz for the last of the assassins charging from the right, dancing the man's flesh in a backpedaling reverse step, and then tapping him into the great beyond with a couple of shots that erased his face in a wash of red surprise. The killer went down and stayed there.

Enemy bullets plowed into the fender of the car behind Katz as the Israeli commando turned to confront the last of their Thai foes. The gunman leading the trio was the same one Katz had winged in the shoulder earlier. His arm dangled uselessly at his side like a broken stalk of celery as the pain-dazed fanatic corrected his aim.

Katzenelenbogen's SIG-Sauer blaster sent a bullet flying into the Thai's chest. The killer grunted as the impact of the 115-grain hollowpoint swept him off of his feet and onto his already injured shoulder. Katz fired again and ended the Thai's brief bout with misery.

Seeing their comrade struck down by the unerring accuracy of the one-armed fiend before them, the final two Thais turned tail and ran, weaving among parked cars, and fleeing pedestrians until they vanished from sight.

As the four Phoenix Force teammates regrouped, Agent Fisher commented, "Some Saturday night date you guys turned out to be. I've heard of some pretty rough action coming down in Potpong, but this takes the cake. We're lucky to be alive."

"Can't say the same for the opposition," Encizo observed. "Looks like we creamed them."

"Except for the two who got away," Katz agreed, then said to McCarter, "I take it you didn't make it to the end of the alley?"

The cockney shook his head. "We met up with four poufs wearing skirts."

"Sounds like you're referring to *kra-toeys*," Fisher said, then went on to explain the true nature of the individuals McCarter and Encizo had encountered. "What about Sutha Nakhon, then? Does this mean the bastard slipped away from us?"

"Somehow, I don't think so," James concluded just as Gary Manning emerged from around a corner.

The brawny Canadian's fist was clamped like a vise around the neck of a demoralized Sutha Nakhon. With Manning calling the shots, the Thai informer and part-time pimp and drug dealer shuffled forward on unsteady legs, his nose mashed awkwardly to the side of his bruised and battered face.

"Sorry I missed all the fireworks," Manning apologized.

"Hey, apology accepted," Fisher was quick to say. "Now that we have Mr. Fleet-of-foot, here, maybe we can find out what the hell's been going on."

## 13

"Captured?" General Ma, whose hearing never missed anything, asked hopefully. "Did I hear you say Sutha Nakhon has been captured?"

"Yes." Colonel Manoon Roopkachorn turned away from the telephone. "Sutha has been captured...."

"Why, that is splendid news!" General Ma clapped his hands. "I confess, Manoon, I had reservations about your people in Bangkok being able to pull it off, but I will be the first to admit that I was wrong."

"Please," Manoon interrupted before the farce could go any farther. "It's true, as I said, that Sutha has been captured... but it is the damned Americans who have him!"

The smile on General Ma's face dissolved. "What?"

"You heard me." Manoon repeated the distressing truth. "The Americans took Sutha Nakhon into their custody less than an hour ago."

"This is terrible," Lo Hsing Han lamented. "It is the very last thing we wanted to happen."

"But what of the people you had searching for Sutha?" General Ma's tongue was not to be stilled.

"And what of those you assured us would take care of the Americans?"

Manoon lowered his head in shame. "Dead. Most of them, anyway. Two of my people escaped with their miserable lives."

"Where did this happen?" Chang Chi-Fu asked.

"In the Potpong district," Manoon replied. "Altogether, fourteen men launched a surprise attack on the Americans as they were leaving a nightclub."

"A surprise that did not work out as planned, it seems," General Ma said, disgusted. "It is a sad day, indeed, when fourteen men cannot dispose of a few American jackals."

"Don't forget they were assisted by the DEA man stationed in Bangkok," Manoon felt obliged to point out.

"Which still means that your men outnumbered the Americans by more than two to one." General Ma was not impressed with Manoon's feeble excuses for failure. The real cause of the defeat of Manoon's people was clearly Manoon's gross inefficiency. "And you say all but a couple of your men were killed?"

Manoon nodded. "It was they who phoned me."

"Hmm." The general settled back into the cushions of his chair. "Next time you see them I would suggest you do the cowards a favor and shoot them."

"Nonsense," Manoon scoffed. "My men are not cowards. If they are all that remains of an original force of fourteen, then I am convinced they gave a good accounting of themselves. Besides, if they had not managed to escape, it would have taken us much longer to learn that Sutha is in American hands.''

''Be that as it may,'' Lo Hsing Han said, in no mood to argue, ''we must now reflect carefully upon our next move. With Sutha the Americans' prisoner, we must assume that he will be interrogated.''

''And being of fine Thai stock,'' Manas stated proudly, ''he will tell the Americans nothing. Personally, I have no qualms whatsoever about the integrity of our operation being breached. Sutha will not betray us.''

General Ma laughed sullenly. ''It is a pity, former Wing Commander Manas Roopkachorn, that all of us cannot share equally your confidence in this known informer, pimp and peddler of narcotics to women and children. If Sutha is interrogated, then it is ridiculous for us to expect that he will not reveal our secrets.''

''Unfortunately,'' Chang said, ''General Ma's point is valid. With all due respect to Sutha Nakhon's record, we must assume the worse—that he will betray us.

''Even if he does not tell the Americans what they want to know, we will be no more worse off for making preparations to ensure our safety, in case Sutha's ability to withstand torture is not as high as Manoon and Manas think.''

''You believe the Americans might subject Sutha to torture, then?'' Manas asked.

Chang answered, ''Why not? It is certainly a possibility.''

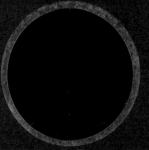

# Terrorists, anarchists, hijackers and drug dealers—BEWARE!

In a world shock-tilted by terror, Mack Bolan and his courageous combat teams, *SOBs* and our new high-powered entry, *Vietnam: Ground Zero* provide America's best hope for salvation.

Fueled by white-hot rage and sheer brute force, they blaze a war of vengeance against a tangled international network of trafficking and treachery. Join them as they battle the enemies of democracy in timely, hard-hitting stories ripped from today's headlines.

## Get 4 explosive novels delivered right to your home—FREE

Return the attached Card, and we'll send you 4 gut-chilling, high-voltage Gold Eagle novels—FREE!

If you like them, we'll send you 6 brand-new books every other month to preview. Always before they're available in stores. Always at a hefty saving off the retail price. Always with the right to cancel and owe nothing.

As a subscriber, you'll also get…
- our free newsletter *AUTOMAG* with each shipment
- special books to preview and buy at a deep discount

## Get a digital quartz calendar watch—FREE

As soon as we receive your Card, we'll send you a digital quartz calendar watch as an outright gift. It comes complete with long-life battery and one-year warranty (excluding battery). *And like the 4 free books, it's yours to keep even if you never buy another Gold Eagle book.*

## RUSH YOUR ORDER TO US TODAY.

PRINTED IN U.S.A.

**Meet America's most potent human weapons**

*Mack Bolan* and his courageous combat squads—*Able Team* & *Phoenix Force*—along with *SOBs* and *Vietnam: Ground Zero* unleash the best sharpshooting firepower ever published. Join them as they blast their way through page after page of raw action toward a fiery climax of rage and retribution.

"Twelve men killed tonight, plus the others slaughtered in the canal this afternoon." Manoon bemoaned the unexpected turn of events. "Where will it end?"

"That depends entirely upon us," Chang told him. "If we blindly ignore what could be coming our way soon, then we have only ourselves to blame. If, however, we prepare for further intervention by the Americans, then I am certain we will quell their interference once and for all.

"And I'm not inclined to label Manoon's men cowards, General Ma. These DEA or CIA hooligans who have made such a nuisance of themselves are not your typical pencil pushers who have grown fat from spending their days sipping alcohol and sitting comfortably upon their backsides. They are highly trained killers, determined to follow through on their investigation to the very end. And what that means is that, unless we stop them, they will eventually find their way to us."

Lo Hsing Han sighed. "A most disturbing proposition. Are we to be reduced to the level of common street brawlers, then?"

"Not at all," Chang told the Burmese Communist Party leader, then amended his statement. "But that is only if we take the proper steps now to protect ourselves."

"You think the Americans will come here to Pattaya?" Manoon asked.

"I am certain of it," Chang replied. "Sutha will talk and the Americans will come, as surely as night follows day. If we accept that this will happen, then there will be no way for the meddling Americans to live beyond their journey to Pattaya.

"They want to find us? Fine. When they roll into town we will make it easy for them to do so. We will coax them, lure them into lowering their defenses and then we will close our trap behind them."

"I cannot believe what I am hearing," General Ma protested. "Don't tell me you actually expect all of us to sit here quietly until our opponents from the United States decide to attack. We have better things to do than waste our valuable time."

"Yes," Lo Hsing Han concurred. "With our opium refinery fully operational for a month now, the five of us are due to fly north to Chiang Mai to supervise the inauguration of the heroin runs to our storage facilities in Khao Soon. We'll be bringing how much heroin with us? Eight tons? And that's only the beginning of what is to follow.

"No, I agree with General Ma. Overseeing the first of our deliveries from our Chiang Mai refinery must not be postponed. There's too much riding on our operation to suffer any kind of unnecessary delay."

"That's not what I was suggesting," Chang said curtly. "When I said we should prepare a special welcome for the Americans when they arrive here, I did not mean that all of us should remain in Pattaya to do so. Quite honestly, I think Manas should be able to handle the arrangements without any help from the rest of us."

Manas made it clear that he did not appreciate being singled out by Chang. "Why me?"

"Why not you?" General Ma butted in. "I don't care what anyone says. It was the gross inefficiency of your brother's people in Bangkok that made such a move necessary in the first place. Unless he's willing to remain behind in Pattaya, then I vote with Chang that the task should fall to you."

Manoon cut the general short. "I'm not afraid of the Americans. If Manas wants to go ahead with the rest of you to Chiang Mai, then I will be happy to stay and settle matters with our American foes. It makes no difference to me."

"Nor to me," General Ma stated with a smirk. "As long as you or your brother handle affairs here in Pattaya, I will be satisfied."

"My brother is not afraid of the Americans, and neither am I," Manas said. "Go to Chiang Mai as planned. There is no reason for the Americans to further jeopardize our plans. If and when they come to Pattaya, I will deal with them."

"Then what are we so upset about?" Lo Hsing Han asked the group, sick to death of the continual bickering between the Roopkachorn brothers and General Ma. Once the heroin deliveries from the north to the south were on something approaching a regular schedule, the BCP commander promised himself that Manoon and Manas and General Ma would be dealt with. Unchecked, such dissension could only spell disaster for their operation.

"If Manas agrees to stay and deal with the Americans," Lo Hsing Han went on, "then I say it is time to turn our attention to the future, instead of dwelling upon the past."

And with that suggestion General Ma could not find fault.

## 14

"This thing is bigger than any of us at the DEA could have guessed," Agent Fisher said, opening the white envelope containing the five photographs and spreading out the pictures on the bare tabletop. "If what Sutha revealed during your interrogation is true, then my job in Thailand is just beginning."

"Trust me, Fisher," Calvin James assured the man. "Sutha wasn't lying to me. I made sure of it."

That was precisely what James had done. When they left the Potpong district behind after the clash with their mysterious Thai assailants, Phoenix Force and the recalcitrant prisoner had been escorted by Fisher to an out-of-the-way office complex on the outskirts of Bangkok, owned and operated by the DEA.

As Manning finished tying the gagged Sutha to a chair, Fisher had asked, "Now what?"

"Now you look like you could stand a short breather," Katz advised. "Call us here every thirty minutes starting an hour from now. We'll let you know when we have something worthwhile."

"Hey, don't go killing the guy," Fisher said, noticing Sutha's eyes widen to saucers. "As much as I'd love to write him off right now, he's the only chance we've got of cracking this thing."

"Please," Katz told him. "We want those secrets as much as you do."

So Fisher had departed, leaving Sutha Nakhon with Phoenix Force for what turned out to be a most informative discussion. At first the broken-nosed criminal tried coming on tough like a Thai version of Little Caesar. When that failed to impress his captors he started to cry. In the end he broke down and told what he claimed was the truth.

"We'll see," James said after Sutha had finished spilling his guts out in a rattling nonstop confession. "For your sake, I hope you're not lying."

"I do not lie," Sutha insisted, his eyes blinking in terror as James unzipped a small Leatherette pouch and removed a hypodermic syringe. "What is the matter with you people? Are you deaf? Can you not understand? Sticking me with needles is not required. I have told you the truth. There is no reason to kill me."

"Shut up," James snapped. "You're lucky this isn't the poison you sell from your office above the lacquerware factory. This won't put you on ice, mister, but it will let us know if you've been trying to run a scam on us." James held up the hypodermic. "This is called scopolamine, a truth serum."

Seeing the needle descend toward his bare arm, Sutha began rocking from side to side in his chair. "No, no, no."

Katz placed the steel hooks of his prosthesis directly under Sutha's chin. "Protesting will only make the procedure more painful. You would be wise to accept your fate. Do we understand each other?"

Sutha gulped as if he were trying to swallow a watermelon whole, and nodded.

"Good," Katz said, then signaled to James. "He's all yours."

Under the influence of the scopolamine, Sutha Nakhon had corroborated all he had confessed to Phoenix Force earlier. When Agent Fisher checked in on the phone, Katz had informed him of this. Now, with the dazed Sutha recovering from his ordeal in an adjacent office, they were going over the wealth of new information they had at their disposal.

"I've heard of this geezer," McCarter said, pointing at a photograph of General Ma. "He was responsible for a lot of the aggro we came up against when I worked in Hong Kong."

"That's no surprise," Fisher said. "General Ma has been in the opium business since 1961. No one else has survived as long, and with the in-fighting that goes on among groups dealing in narcotics, that's quite an accomplishment."

"What's this character's story?" Encizo picked up another photograph.

"Lo Hsing Han is leader of the Burmese Communist Party," answered Fisher. "He has about ten or twelve thousand men under his command."

Manning whistled softly. "Nothing like stacking the deck in your favor, is there?"

"That's not the half of it," Fisher went on. "In addition to his regular troops, we think Lo Hsing Han also has access to a thirty-thousand-man militia. Han and his boys were recently booted out of Burma. The DEA had been wondering when and where he would eventually surface. Now we know."

Fisher tapped a third photo. "Chang Chi-Fu is the new kid on the block. He's only been active in production and distribution of heroin since 1975. Even so, his rise to the top has been meteoric. As things stand today, along with his private army of supporters, known locally as the San United Army, Chang personally controls more than a third of the world's heroin supply."

"And unless I'm incorrect," James offered, "Chang is the honcho I've heard referred to as the king of the opium trade."

"One and the same," Fisher said. "The man's a snake."

"Where do the two brothers fit in?" McCarter asked. "All Sutha kept repeating was that they represented Thailand's only hope for the future—that, plus the fact that it was Manoon Roopkachorn who ordered him to arrange the phony meeting with the four DEA agents who were killed."

"Manoon and Manas both participated in Thailand's most recent unsuccessful coup attempt," Fisher said. "Many of their associates are now behind bars and awaiting trial for their treasonous acts, but Manoon and Manas escaped unharmed. It's not readily admitted, but the brothers have considerable support from a segment of the population."

"So," James summed up, "the way Sutha tells it, all these different personalities are now working together with the common goal of putting the Golden Triangle's entire heroin operation under one roof. That was why your DEA buddies were killed—Chang and his pals wanted to keep the Royal Thai government preoccupied with gripes from Uncle Sam while they got their program going full swing here. Their scheme worked up to a point, but then we entered the picture. Now we've given Chang and company something else to think about."

"Did Sutha tell you where we can find Chang and the rest?" Fisher asked.

"Yes," Katz said. "Since the night your agents were murdered, Chang and his friends have been engaged in a series of meetings south of here in the city of Pattaya."

"Did Sutha say where in Pattaya the meetings were being held?"

"Sutha's never actually been there," Katz replied, "but he says it's a warehouse that's been converted into a base of operations that enables Chang and his partners to meet and conduct business openly, without having to fear the kind of interference they could expect if they set up shop in Bangkok.''

"Wonderful," Fisher said. "Now all I need to do is inform my people what you've learned, then hightail it down to Pattaya and mop up the place with those bastards.''

"Whoa!" Katz said. "Slow down a minute. Sure, we all agree the information Sutha's given us should be put to use, but bowing out of the picture at this stage of the game isn't how we operate. We have every intention of following this mission through to its logical conclusion.''

"What's that supposed to mean?" Fisher sounded offended.

"This is the part of the movie where you and the DEA go for popcorn," James told him. "We'll handle the situation in Pattaya on our own. Surely now that you've seen us in action, you don't doubt our ability to do so.''

"How could I?" Fisher said. "But hell, it was the execution of my friends that brought you guys to Thailand in the first place. And now you're telling me you don't want the DEA to be in Pattaya for the final kill?''

"You got it," Katz said. "Nor do we want your people to have the slightest idea that Chang and his bunch are even involved, or that they're using Pattaya as a home base. All that is privileged information, and it's to go no farther than this room.

"I realize it's not your fault, but we've already been attacked twice while you were with us—a fairly good indication that someone here in Bangkok has been keeping an eye on you. Up to now your help has been valuable, no doubt about it, but continuing to work with you is a liability we can no longer afford.

"Spilling Sutha's news to your associates is no good, either. Do that and pretty soon the Royal Thai government will get into the act. The stage isn't big enough for that many actors, I'm afraid. Any more players at this point would just be in our way. So you'll simply have to keep all of this to yourself. You were instructed by Washington to follow my orders."

"I know that," Fisher said with a sigh, "but—oh, hell, okay. I don't particularly like it, but you've got my word. I tell nobody what I know."

"I understand what keeping this to yourself must mean to you, Fisher," Katz said. "Thank you."

"Yeah, well, thank me later," Fisher said. "After you deal with the mob in Pattaya."

"We'll do that," Katz said. "In the meantime, maybe you can find a nice cozy place for Sutha while we're gone."

"No problem." Fisher took out a card and scribbled some numbers on the back of it. "Here's where I can be reached if you need to get in touch with me," he said, passing the card to Katz. The Israeli accepted the card and slipped it into his pocket. "We'll try to call anyway to let you know how things turn out."

"You do that," Fisher said. "And whatever you guys do when you reach Pattaya, play it close to the vest. Don't take any chances. Chang and his friends are animals when it comes to dealing with their enemies. They don't fuck around."

Katz grimly said in tones laced with ice, "Neither do we."

**15**

Renting a car at noon on Sunday, Phoenix Force made the eighty-five mile journey from Bangkok to Pattaya in less than two hours. As they traveled along Sukhumvit Highway, they welcomed the moments of peace the trip provided.

Calvin James was the only one of the five who had visited Pattaya previously on an R&R excursion while he was stationed in Vietnam. From what James could see as they entered the outskirts of the popular Thai resort area, the Eastern Gulf Coast city had changed enormously.

Before there had been only a few hotels; now almost one hundred hotels, bars and restaurants sporting names like Hank's Hideaway, Bonanza Court and Nautical Inn vied for the valuable real estate along the beautiful white beaches. Pattaya was a perfect example of city planning at its most commercial.

Although they had no intention of spending the night in Pattaya, Phoenix Force drove to the Royal Cliff Beach Hotel and checked into rooms they had reserved before leaving Bangkok. They hoped they appeared to be tourists expecting to enjoy Pattaya's many attractions.

They checked into their rooms and secured the doors with special locking devices developed by North America International, the company Manning worked for as a security consultant. Phoenix Force then set out to verify the information they had wrung out of Sutha Nakhon. Yakov Katzenelenbogen had not been entirely truthful with Agent Fisher regarding the Thai informer's scopolamine-induced confession. While it was true that Sutha had revealed Pattaya as the location of the enemy's base of operations, the story about the base being a converted warehouse was pure fabrication on the Israeli's part.

As much as Katz wanted to believe that the DEA special agent would keep his word and not reveal the particulars of Sutha's confession to his superiors, Katz had learned from hard experience never to divulge any more information to outsiders than was absolutely necessary.

The five men returned to their rental car in the Royal Cliff's parking lot and drove back out to Sukhumvit Highway, where they turned right. In less than ten minutes Encizo pulled their car to a halt beneath a row of palm trees facing the beach. The waters of the Eastern Gulf gleamed magnificently, reflecting a rainbow of colors in the afternoon sunshine. Away in the distance Pattaya's offshore islands shimmered and danced upon the blue liquid carpet.

"All ashore who's going ashore," Encizo announced, shutting off the engine and climbing out.

As they began to walk along in the shade of the coconut palms James said, "It's a damn shame when you stop to think about it, how a few rotten apples can spoil the image of an entire country. If I was merely going on the experiences we've had since we arrived here yesterday, and didn't know better, I'd have to say the Thais are by and large a mean-spirited people. But nothing could be farther from the truth. With the exception of the fools who were stupid enough to try to kill us, most Thais I've met have been warm, open and extremely friendly."

"There's good and bad to be found in every culture," Katz responded. "When it comes to the problems of narcotics trafficking in Thailand, the real offenders are not the Thais, but are generally Chinese who have settled in Thailand, as well as other nationals from neighboring countries."

"Speaking of which," McCarter cut in, "if this Chang Chi-Fu and his pals are aware that we captured Sutha Nakhon last night, then they have to figure Nakhon would try to save his hide by giving us the rundown on their setup here in Pattaya."

"And that means Chang and company could be expecting us to pay them a visit," Manning said.

"We'll see that we don't disappoint them, then," Katz stated.

They reached the last of the coconut palms and began following a path of cracked concrete that took them to the top of a low-rising hill. There the path ended at a stone stairway, which led downward. Rather than continuing, however, Katz and McCarter sat down on the top step, while Manning, Encizo and James stood by, all of them apparently drinking in the splendid view of the gulf.

McCarter took out a cigarette and brought a match to its tip. "Well, mates, there she is," he said, inhaling the smoke. "I know you could say I've been wrong in the past, but from where I sit, we're talking a piece a cake. We'll be in and out before they know what's hit them."

What they were actually looking at was a four-story beachfront hotel. The Asians Arms was about fifty yards away at the end of a red-brick walkway that extended from the bottom of the stone stairway.

Unlike many Pattaya hotels that featured two hundred or more rooms, the Asian Arms was a throwback to a bygone era when quality and style were not dependent on air-conditioning, the size or shape of the swimming pool or the proximity of the ice machine.

The hotel had twenty-five suites to choose from, the finest of which occupied more than half the fourth floor. Each suite had a private balcony offering splendid views of the lovely Pattaya coastline.

A small parking lot was within walking distance of the main entrance. At present five automobiles were parked in the lot: two Jaguar XJ6s, a Rolls-Royce Silver Spur, a BMW 735i and a Mercedez-Benz 190E.

"Somebody's living right," Encizo observed. "And Sutha gave us a good idea where the money for those fancy wheels came from."

"A place this nice and cozy," Manning said, "you'd think would be booked up year-round."

"I suppose it's possible that the rest of the guests are in Pattaya this afternoon taking in the sights," James suggested. "Still, Gary has a point. The busiest tourist season here doesn't hit for about another month, but even so there should be more cars parked in the lot."

"I agree," Katz said. "Something isn't right here."

"You guys get the feeling we're being watched?" Manning asked.

"Like we're the stars of our own program on the telly," McCarter said. "Top floor balcony, facing us, behind the sliding glass doors. I saw a curtain move."

Encizo took a look without being obvious about it. "Yeah, David, you're right. It looks like— Hey, what now?"

As they watched, the curtain was pulled aside and the sliding glass doors opened. A man they all recognized stepped casually onto the balcony, apparently to stretch and grab a breath of fresh air.

McCarter finished his cigarette and stood. "As I live and breathe, if it isn't former Wing Commander Manas Roopkachorn. What a surprise."

"I think we've seen enough." Katz stood, too.

As if they had nothing more on their minds than a casual stroll back to their car, the Stony Man five turned and slowly retraced their steps to where Encizo had parked their vehicle.

"No doubt about it," Manning said as they walked. "They know we're here."

"Bloody right, they do," McCarter said. "Old Manas wasn't strutting on the balcony for his health. He's using himself as bait to lure us into whatever trap he has planned for us."

"Traps can be a lot like guns," James noted. "Sometimes they backfire."

WATCHING THE FIVE MEN disappear over the rim of the hill, Manas Roopkachorn turned and strode confidently back into his suite.

"It worked," he told the twelve men gathered inside. "The Americans saw me. I am sure of it."

"And yet they have departed?" asked a wiry Thai whose name was Opas Panyavit. "They saw you and did not come nearer to investigate?"

"These men are jackals," Manas said. "They are cowards without the courage to carry out their criminal acts under the scrutiny of the sun. They have seen me, though, and they will be back. Once darkness has fallen they will return."

"And then what?" Opas questioned eagerly.

"Why, what do you think?" Manas smiled. "We will be waiting for them."

## 16

The two men were sitting inside the Rolls-Royce Silver Spur, which was parked in front of the Asian Arms Hotel.

"I am bored," droned Udom Sengchanh, toying with the submachine gun resting upon his lap. "It has been four hours since I last stretched my legs or was allowed to relieve my bladder."

"Ha!" Tanee Jansuwan said. "You'll just have to exercise a little patience. I told you not to drink so much when we were having dinner."

"I know. But who thought at the time that the Americans would wait so long to attack? Don't they know we have better things to do than to stake out the front of the hotel all night? If you ask me, the Americans have changed their minds about coming. I know Manas expects them to attack, but this time I believe he is wrong."

"How you or I feel about the matter makes no difference one way or the other," Tanee insisted. "All we are expected to do is follow orders, and right now our instructions are to sit and wait for the Americans. If we are still waiting at sunrise, and the Americans still have not shown, at least no one will be able to accuse us of not obeying our orders. Now, if you have nothing more to say, I would appreciate not having to listen to further complaints."

Udom drummed his fingers over his SMG as sweat trickled down the back of his neck. "It is too hot in here."

"So, what am I now? The weatherman?"

"The windows are steaming up. How can we watch for the Americans if we cannot see out the windows?"

"I can see perfectly," said Tanee, who was sitting behind the wheel of the Silver Spur. "Perhaps if you did not exercise your mouth so much, the windows on your side of the car would not be so steamy."

Udom nodded at the foggy windshield. "Why not turn on the defrost for a minute or two?"

"What? Are you serious? It would make too much noise. Wipe the glass with the palm of your hand if you must."

But Udom was not prepared to give up so easily. "If I do, and the Americans happen to be looking, then they will know we are hiding in the car. Please, Tanee, I am about to suffocate. If you will not turn on the defrost for me, then please roll down the window to let in some fresh air."

"It is cool outside."

"And an oven inside," Udom countered. "Please."

Tanee murmured something under his breath and reached for the key in the ignition. "Oh, all right, I will put the windows down, but only for a few minutes. If Manas thinks we are enjoying ourselves too much out here, there will be hell to pay later."

Tanee turned the key to power the automatic windows, then depressed the switch to roll them all the way down. "There." He nodded to Udom and whispered, "Fresh air. I hope you are satisfied."

"Thank you," Udom said sullenly. "I feel better already."

Faster than either of the sentries would have dreamed possible, they were dead men. Powerful arms flashed through the open windows on both sides of the Rolls. Calvin James swept his forearm around and under the chin of the man behind the steering wheel, simultaneously lifting and pulling him from his seat.

Knowing the sentry would have to be dealt with before he could alert his friends inside the Asian Arms, the black commando brought up his forearm and tilted the man's chin toward the roof of the car. It only dawned on the doomed guard that he was about to die when the G-96 Boot 'n' Belt knife in James's left hand flapped open a gurgling path across the soft exposed flesh of his throat.

Blood washed freely from the terrible wound as James withdrew the G-96's double-edged blade. He held his right hand over the dying sentry's mouth to smother the screams that bubbled like a nightmare beneath his palm. Then the guard's body contorted with one mighty spasm and was still.

Rafael Encizo disposed of the second guard with equal speed and skill, using his Gerber Mark I knife to slash the man's throat in a fluid motion of instant death. By the time Encizo resheathed his weapon the sentry was dead.

James and Encizo exchanged knowing glances, then moved as silently as death across the darkened parking lot to the main entrance of the Asian Arms. None of the suites faced the parking lot, so the Cuban and his partner reached their goal undetected. The glass opened and the two Phoenix soldiers vanished inside.

Observing the actions of his colleagues from the top of the stone stairway that overlooked the hotel, and viewing their progress through the Starlite nightscope affixed to his H&K G-3 SG-1 sniper rifle, Gary Manning commented softly to Katz, "They're in."

"Good," Katz said. "They'll have a few minutes to get upstairs before David lets Manas Roopkachorn and the rest of us know that party time has arrived."

Sequestered in the larger of their two suites at the Royal Cliff Beach Hotel, Phoenix Force had worked out the details of their late-night strike. They put their plan to work shortly after midnight. Under cover of darkness the Asian Arms resembled anything but the top choice on anyone's list of vacation spots.

For starters, none of the floodlights dotting the parking lot were on. Also, the same five cars were parked in the lot. It seemed unlikedly that legitimate guests were staying at the hotel.

Fueling the Stony Man crew's suspicion that Manas Roopkachorn was bringing new meaning to the term "tourist trap" was the fact that all the lights over the hotel entrance were turned off, too. The invitation to them to enter the Asian Arms was obvious. Manas was making it too easy.

When they arrived at the hotel Gary Manning had had no trouble using his Starlite scope to pick out the two Thai sentries holding the fort in the Rolls-Royce. Nor had it been any problem for the Canadian warrior to locate another pair of guards concealed high on the dunes on the opposite side of the hotel.

McCarter went after the duo hiding in the dunes. The Londoner crept silently toward the pair, his Ingram MAC-10 held ready. The machine-pistol was equipped with a foot-long sound suppressor for delivering death with a minimum of noise. He moved closer, ready to take out both opponents with well-placed bullets to the base of their skulls.

The Briton did not like killing men this way. He preferred a face-to-face confrontation. A fair fight. But this was war, and sometimes one had to break the rules of fair play in combat. Besides, there was too much at stake. The trade these men had chosen was far more immoral than anything McCarter or the other men of Phoenix Force would ever dream of doing.

Suddenly one of the Thai gunmen turned his head. His eyes widened when he saw McCarter. He started to swing his American-made M-3 greasegun toward the Briton. The silenced Ingram coughed a trio of muffled rounds and the Thai's face exploded into a crimson glob.

The other Thai killer jumped up, holding his weapon, an M-16 assault rifle, in his fists. The frame of the rifle formed a solid bar as it struck McCarter's Ingram. The machine-pistol hopped from the Briton's grasp and the Thai immediately struck at the Phoenix fighter's head with the rifle butt.

McCarter ducked. The hard plastic stock whistled over his head as he rammed a solid punch to the Thai's solar plexus. The man groaned, and McCarter drove his left fist under the Thai's rib cage as he shuffled away from a clumsy attempt to push the rifle butt in his face.

A karate chop to the base of the skull stunned the Thai. McCarter swiftly seized the man from behind and hammered a knee to the Thai's kidney, then grabbed the M-16 and pulled it toward his opponent. His kick to the back of the knee buckled the Thai's leg and threw him off balance. The man fell to his knees as McCarter pulled the frame of the M-16 across his throat.

With his knee planted at the small of the Thai's spine, McCarter hauled back on the rifle frame. The gunman tried to pry the steel from his throat, but his strength was rapidly ebbing. He reached back, trying to claw at McCarter's eyes. The Briton shoved hard, driving the steel frame of the rifle into his opponent's throat. The man's windpipe collapsed. For a moment his body stiffened, then it went limp in McCarter's grasp. The Briton released the rifle and let the corpse slump to the ground.

By now, McCarter knew that James and Encizo would have eliminated the guards in the Rolls. It was the Briton's cue to penetrate the Asian Arms.

McCarter found the gunman inside the lobby. Overconfidence had made the Thai guard careless. He was sitting on the floor, his back against a wall, submachine gun resting between his knees. He held a penlight as he glanced at the pages of a movie magazine.

McCarter moved within two feet of the man and whispered, "Shhh." Then his shoe caved in the side of the man's skull with deadly accuracy. Vertebrae snapped and the gunman's head lolled around in a lazy circle of death.

McCarter made his exit from the reception area just as Calvin James and Rafael Encizo scurried away from the outline of the Rolls, heading across the parking lot in his direction. The British commando nodded in satisfaction. Ignoring the elevator, he darted through a doorway that led to a stairwell. Noiselessly, McCarter began to climb.

He took two steps at a time, like a jungle cat on the prowl. No sound betrayed his passage. At the second floor he tested the door leading off the stairwell, nudging it open a fraction of an inch.

He saw nothing but an empty, dimly lit hallway. He listened intently, but heard nothing out of the ordinary. Finally, he closed the door and resumed his climb, repeating his inspection procedure on the third floor. It, too, was deserted.

At the fourth floor he heard them—two or more men's voices, talking in Thai just beyond the stairwell door. Then the voices gradually faded.

His Ingram MAC-10 held at the ready, McCarter pressed his fingertips to the surface of the door and pushed, opening it just enough to let him see out onto the fourth floor. A trio of Thai gunmen occupied the hallway, their backs to McCarter as they walked toward the elevator.

McCarter allowed the door to close. Letting his Ingram hang by its lanyard, he withdrew a pair of hand grenades from his coat pockets. One was a ball-shaped M-33 fragmentation grenade, the other an M-8 smoke grenade. McCarter pulled the pin of the M-33 first, holding down its safety lever with his left hand. In similar fashion he quickly readied the M-8.

McCarter tensed and listened, to make sure the Thais were still moving toward the elevator. Assured that they were, he pushed open the door and lobbed both grenades into the hallway. He was halfway down to the third floor when the M-33 exploded.

"WHAT IS HAPPENING?" Manas Roopkachorn demanded as the unexpected explosion rocked the corridor just outside his personal suite.

"We are under attack!" shouted Opas Panyavit.

"Impossible," Manas snarled. He grabbed for his L-2 A-3 Sterling submachine gun as the sliding glass doors leading to the balcony suddenly shattered under the impact of a storm of bullets.

Sprayed by shards of flying glass, one of Manas's men pressed his fingers to his bleeding face and ran screaming around the room, charging blindly in a headlong rush that carried him crashing into a wall. A tremor convulsed the shrieking man's body and his screams abruptly ceased.

Someone tried to open the door to the suite. Manas was the first to react to this latest threat, spinning on his heel and firing his Sterling as he completed his turn. He squeezed off half his weapon's 38-round magazine before his panic left him. Still covering the ruined door with his SMG, he motioned to Opas.

"Open the door," he ordered.

Opas gulped and did as instructed, turning the knob and pulling the door open with a rapid jerk of his wrist. Manas shuddered when he saw the multilated body of one of his own men tumble into the room.

"It is Govit!" Opas exclaimed as if he had just seen a ghost. "He was trying to get into the room and you killed him, Manas!"

"Ridiculous!" Manas defended his actions. "How was I to know it was Govit? Did he call out to let us know he was there? No! Besides, look at the condition of his body. He is cut from top to bottom, and not from machine gun bullets, either."

Opas risked a glance through the open doorway and reported the horrible sight that met his eyes. "Charoon and Thawee are both dead, too." Then Opas pointed to the far end of the hallway. "But look! There is smoke. It must be from the explosion that killed our men. The Asian Arms is on fire!"

Manas shoved the excited Opas out of the way to confirm the worst. "Opas is right," he announced to the remaining three gunmen in the suite. "There is a fire burning down by the stairwell. Already the smoke from the blaze is spilling this way."

"We are doomed," one of the Thais insisted. "We will be roasted alive!"

"Not if we fight our way downstairs," Manas countered, wishing deep in his heart that he had not permitted the wily General Ma to trick him into staying on in Pattaya on his own. "Bring your weapons and follow me! To delay is to die!"

Manas and his men filed from the room as the stinging smoke from McCarter's M-8 grenade irritated their eyes and lungs. Coughing and wiping away their tears, they stumbled to the elevator. None of them paused in their panicked flight long enough to wonder why the "fire" supposedly raging on the hotel's fourth floor generated no heat.

Manas reached the elevator first and thanked whatever gods were watching over him that the doors to the lift were open. He dived into the elevator and pushed the button for the lobby as the rest of his men rushed in, too.

"How could we be attacked?" Opas was dumbfounded. "What of the others who were guarding the hotel out front? Why did they not protect us?"

"Silence!" Manas commanded. "Conserve your strength."

Then the doors slid shut and the elevator began its descent to the lobby.

David McCarter raced down the stairs, making no attempt to mask the noise. He hit the third-floor landing just as the muffled chatter of autofire filtered into the stairwell from above. Good. The grenade he had thrown had done its work well; Manas and his cronies were shooting at windmills. Now, all Roopkachorn and his friends had to do was take the M-8 smoke grenade at its face value, and the lobby of the Asian Arms would become the most popular place in the hotel.

McCarter reached the second floor, then was once more at ground level. As he approached the door leading into the lobby, he heard Encizo from the opposite side.

"If that's not you, McCarter, you're a dead man," warned the Cuban.

"Guess it's my lucky day, then," McCarter returned, stepping through the doorway.

"What's the word on the guests upstairs?" James asked.

"I heard some shooting after I threw the grenades," McCarter answered, "but that's about it. I was long gone, which means they're either shooting at shadows or one another. Either way we win.''

''Any idea how many unfriendlies we're talking about?'' Encizo wanted to know.

''Enough to take a ride in the lift,'' McCarter said. ''We'll be able to count them as they come out.''

McCarter, James and Encizo spread out, concealing themselves but maintaining an unrestricted view of the elevator doors. Lighted numbers above the doors were counting down from four to one. A bell chimed as the number one glowed. The doors to the elevator parted and four Thai gunmen stormed into the lobby.

Raking his weapon from side to side in a bid to clear the lobby of anyone seeking to prevent his escape, the first gunner out of the lift stopped dead where he stood as Encizo's MP-5 machine pistol effectively erased most of the man's features in a telling 3-round burst of fire. The nearly headless body remained upright for several heartbeats, then collapsed on the lobby floor.

McCarter dived behind the reception desk as a flurry of enemy slugs did their best to reduce the area to splinters. Sawdust still filled the air when the pair who had tried to mow down McCarter made a desperate dash across the lobby for the exit.

Convinced they were going to reach their goal unscathed, the Thai duo learned otherwise the hard way when Calvin James suddenly appeared from behind a stone pillar with his S&W M-76. Both Thai gunmen danced around like drops of water sizzling on a skillet. Then James quit shooting, and the pair's bullet-inspired movements ended.

McCarter rose from behind the remains of the reception desk as the last gunman out of the elevator yelled something at the top of his voice and charged at James in a blind rage.

"Later, sunshine," McCarter pronounced, bringing his Ingram to life, squeezing back on the MAC-10's trigger as Encizo's Heckler and Koch joined the deadly celebration.

Caught in the relentless cross fire from the two Phoenix Force soldiers, the Thai gunman died blasting twin holes in the ceiling with his double-barreled shotgun. The noise from his last hurrah was still reverberating when James called out.

"Easy, fellas," the black commando warned, stepping again behind the pillar. "We're still missing the ringleaders of this show." He paused, then said louder, "How about it, Manas? Are you ready to surrender?"

"Go to hell!" the Thai's voice shot back from inside and to the right of the elevator's open doors. "I surrender to no CIA dogs! Never!"

"Where is your brother, Manas?" James asked. "And Chang, General Ma and Lo Hsing Han? Where are they hiding?"

"Somewhere where you will never find them," the unseen Manas replied uneasily.

"Throw out your weapon and come out of the elevator with your hands in the air," James instructed.

"It's your only chance. All of your men are dead, Manas. Surrender to us now unless you are in a hurry to join them."

"Never!" Manas shouted, and then he was running from the elevator with his Sterling submachine gun blazing a path of temporary freedom before him, a path that ended abruptly as Katzenelenbogen appeared in the entrance to the lobby and used his Uzi SMG to polish the former wing commander off the face of the earth.

Manas cried out as the Israeli's bullets slammed like an invisible freight train into his chest, knocking him from his feet and sending him in an unintentional slide across the floor. His fingers opened and the L-2 A-3 submachine gun slipped away. Manas worked his mouth and died with his brother's name frozen on his lips.

Katz came the rest of the way into the lobby.

"Where's Manning?" McCarter asked.

"Bringing our car around," Katz answered. "Did we bag any of the big shots besides Manas?"

"No dice," Encizo answered. "Manas here is the whole ball of wax. Chang and the rest must have taken a powder for parts unknown long before we got here."

"Damn," Katz swore.

"So, where's that leave us?" James asked.

Katz answered with one word. "Bangkok."

## 17

"Manas is dead," Manoon Roopkachorn repeated, as though doing so would make the horrible truth easier to accept. But it was useless. The ache caused by his loss could not have been worse if he had let a starving rat feed upon his heart. "My brother is dead."

"Casualties are a by-product of any war," General Ma stated.

Manoon, who would have liked nothing more than to put a loaded gun to General Ma's head, responded by saying, "That may be, General, but in this instance my brother should not have been asked to fight the war on his own."

"Nonsense," General Ma said. "You'll have to do better than that, I'm afraid. Manas was hardly left in Pattaya on his own. He had…how many, a dozen men to back him up? And what of their fate? Not a single one survived the fight that claimed your brother's life.

"I understand your feelings, Manoon, but your comments are clouded by emotion. Admit it. Putting Manas in charge of dealing with the Americans was a mistake. He failed. He botched it. It is no good pointing the finger of blame at any of the rest of us, Manoon. The true reason for our failure in Pattaya lies much closer to home.''

Manoon smirked. ''It is easy to be brave when one has his opulent backside planted hundreds of miles from the scene of the battle.''

''Wrong though you may be, you are, of course, entitled to your opinion,'' General Ma said calmly, refusing to allow Manoon to bait him into a full-fledged argument. ''Perhaps, if your experience had some substance to it, and represented more than childish games played out against a backdrop of failed coups, then yours would be an opinion I could respect. Unfortunately, this miracle is not likely to happen.''

''Gentlemen, please.'' Chang Chi-Fu interrupted to restore order to their discussion. ''I really must insist that we set aside our personal differences and concentrate on ensuring that the setbacks we have experienced in Bangkok, and more recently in Pattaya, do not somehow continue to harass us here in Chiang Mai.''

''I don't really see that as a problem,'' Lo Hsing Han said. ''With Manas and everyone else in Pattaya lost, then any connection the Americans might be able to make to the rest of us has been effectively destroyed. With no one to guide them to us, the Americans will wander in circles.''

''What about Sutha Nakhon?'' General Ma asked Manoon. ''That bastard is the real culprit responsible for Manas getting killed, and you know it. So what's to stop him from betraying us yet a second time to the persistant American demons?''

"Simply this," Manoon answered. "Sutha cannot tell the Americans what he does not know. His overview of our entire operation is sketchy at best. I made sure of that. He has a vague idea of what our plans are, but he does not have access to the innermost secrets of our partnership.

"Of course, Sutha knew about our meeting in Pattaya, but this is and was the extent of his knowledge of our comings and goings. I have long followed a policy of selective restriction when issuing information to inferiors. Sutha Nakhon was no exception to that rule. I can assure all of you that he has no idea where our refinery is hidden.''

General Ma smiled thinly. "Does that mean you are willing to guarantee that our troubles with the Americans are over? That we have seen the last of these meddlers from the United States?''

"Though my talents are many, General Ma," Manoon said, "predicting the future is not one of them. Whether the Americans will be satisfied with murdering my brother, and leave the rest of us alone, I cannot say. I know only that they will learn nothing more from Sutha Nakhon.''

"With all respect to your late brother, Manoon," Chang mentioned, "there may be a positive aspect to Manas's unfortunate encounter with the Americans that we are overlooking.''

"What possible good could come from my brother's death?" Manoon demanded. "Manas willingly sacrificed his life for our cause. Isn't that enough?"

"Of course," Chang admitted. "But the incident in Pattaya is certain to fire the imagination of the Thai public for some time to come. The short announcement we heard on the radio is only the beginning. Newspaper and television reporters will all want a piece of the story.

"Manas was, after all, not without his own notoriety. His death is sure to spark an investigation by the Royal Thai government. And with the numerous headaches the government is already experiencing— including explaining to the United States the deaths of the four American narcotics agents—the last thing they want right now is another headache."

Manoon stared blankly at Chang. "My question still stands, Chang. What possible good do we derive from my brother's death?"

"I would think the answer would be obvious even to you, Manoon," General Ma interjected. "With the Royal Thai government distracted by the mystery behind Mannas's death, any interference we might anticipate from them is reduced. In a manner of speaking, by his failure at Pattaya Manas has done the rest of us a favor."

"That remains to be seen," Manoon told General Ma sourly.

## 18

Agent Fisher was not a happy man.

"You guys got a lot of nerve coming here," he said as Phoenix Force entered his three-room apartment.

McCarter crossed uninvited to the kitchen and opened the refrigerator door. "After all we've been through, mate, that's hardly the welcome we were expecting." McCarter rummaged around until he located a can of Coca-Cola Classic hiding behind a bottle of Thai beer. "We thought you'd be glad to see us."

"Why should I be?" Fisher complained. "I'm sorry, but with all that bullshit you dished up about the converted warehouse in Pattaya that the Roopkachorn brothers and their pals were using for their headquarters down south, this is as good a welcome as you get."

"Yes, well, save the injured ego for later," Katz told him. "What good would it have done you to know in advance that Manas and the others were using Pattaya's Asian Arms Hotel as a base of operations?"

"None, but that's not the point," Agent Fisher snapped.

"Of course, it is," the Israeli countered. "Just because you've been on our side in a couple of heated gunfights with the opposition doesn't automatically entitle you to the key to our hearts. Okay? That isn't how we operate and, I suspect deep down, you know it. This is a dangerous world we live in. To do our job and stay alive, we have no choice but to take every precaution."

"Yeah, yeah, I'm not dumb," Fisher said. "You guys gotta be careful, I know. In your line of work, like mine, enemies are damn easy to come by. The way you tell it, though, I should feel lucky you told me you were going to Pattaya in the first place."

Katz shrugged. "That was information you could have learned anyway from questioning Sutha Nakhon."

"Who says I didn't?" Fisher asked. "Sutha talked plenty after the five of you took off, including mentioning the Asian Arms Hotel. Naturally, hearing the truth from him instead of from you pissed me off."

"I thought as much," Katz said. "Where is Sutha now?"

"Cooling his heels with a few of my DEA buddies on the other side of town," Fisher reported, seeming less irritated now about not being taken into Phoenix Force's full confidence. "Until we decide what to do with him. I doubt if he'll give us any hassles. He knows we're aware of his involvement in the deaths of

Dick Warren and the rest at Bang Kwang. He knows that we'd just love an excuse to pound his face into the ground."

"Good," Manning said. "What about local reaction to the Pattaya business?"

"As far as the DEA is concerned," Fisher answered, "you got high marks all around. Our only gripe was that Manas was the only one out of the top big shots you managed to bag. No ideas on where the others disappeared to, I suppose?"

"No," Katz replied. "And that's the truth. We tried to get Manas to surrender, but he refused. He left us no option but to deal with him as we did. And he took the secret of where his brother and the others are hiding to his grave with him."

"Hell," Fisher said. "And Sutha doesn't have anything else to add. I asked. Evidently, Manoon Roopkachorn didn't trust him enough to tell him everything—a wise move on his part as it turns out."

"How about the government's reaction to Pattaya?" Encizo asked.

"Nothing official has come down the pike, yet," Fisher answered, "but word has it that the Royal Thai government is applauding the actions of the 'unnamed' patriotic Thais responsible for bringing former Wing Commander Manas to justice. They don't have a clue who really pulled off the strike against Manas, and right now they don't care. All they care about is that the timing of the incident has worked to their advantage.

"Thailand has been politically unstable ever since Manas and Manoon failed in their attempted coup. The RTG plays down this unrest, of course, but it's there just the same. To the government's way of thinking having Manas meet such a violent end will help put the lid on coups for a long time to come."

"It's nice to know the government won't come looking for us, then," Manning said.

"If they did," Fisher told the brawny Canadian, "it would be to give all you guys medals."

"Is there anything else you think we should know?" Katz asked.

"Just this: the United States has filed a formal protest over the deaths of our dead DEA agents. The Royal Thai government responded by issuing a communiqué to Washington stating that they regretted the four deaths as much as the U.S., and that they're doing everything within their power to see to it that the perpetrators are found and dealt with.

"Unofficially," Fisher continued, "the government's special investigators haven't a clue where to start looking for the killers, and they aren't apt to get much of a push from their superiors, either. With the dust of the last coup still settling, the government has more important things on its mind than the unexplained deaths of four American narcotics agents."

"Which means the government makes a show of tracking down the killers, but actually does squat," James concluded.

Fisher nodded. "You got it."

The telephone in the corner of Fisher's living room rang and he caught it on the second ring.

"Hello?" he answered, listening to the caller, and then said, "Hold on." Fisher covered the mouthpiece and said to the Phoenix Force. "Which one of you guys has an Uncle Saul?"

Katz stood and went to the phone. "I'll take it." He placed the receiver to his ear. "Uncle Saul, how nice of you to call."

"How is everybody doing?" Hal Brognola asked from half a world away. "I understand the weather has been fairly warm since your arrival."

"Nothing we haven't been able to handle," Katz commented.

Although transmissions in and out of Stony Man were routed through a special communications satellite outfitted with a scrambler, neither Brognola nor Katzenelenbogen cared to take any risks with the line.

"I take it that you've been doing some house cleaning during your visit?"

"Only one of the rooms we wanted to clean is spotless," Katz said. "The rest of the house is still very dirty."

"That's too bad. How many rooms altogether are we talking about?" Brognola asked.

"Four."

"I understand," the Fed said, knowing from what Katz told him that only one of a total of five individuals behind the DEA agents' murders had been put permanently on ice. "And when do you hope to get the remaining four rooms clean?"

"That's difficult to say. We might have lost the key to the house in room number one."

"I might be able to recommend a good locksmith, then."

"How's that?"

Brognola said something unintelligible as interference crackled loudly over the line.

"Say that again?" Katz requested after the line had cleared.

"I said, I know a good locksmith who recently quit his job and bought a chemical company in California. Business was bad until he received a one-in-a-million order from an overseas customer. The order was for a terrifically large shipment of acetic anhydride."

"Um-hmm." Katz digested this last piece of information. "And you say it's being shipped here to Bangkok?"

"That's how it reads on the dotted line. The shipment was scheduled to reach Don Muang International roughly three hours ago your time."

"And the particulars of that delivery?" Katz asked. He listened and copied down the pertinent information regarding the flight bringing the shipment of acetic anhydride into Thailand.

"Got it," Katz said once Brognola was finished. "Is there anything else?"

"That should do it," Brognola said. "Good luck on that upcoming cleaning job. If you have no objections, I'll share your news with my neighbor, the one in the white house. He always likes to hear how you're doing. I'll tell him you've got a handle on the situation, no problem at all."

"More like a broom handle," Katz said. "We're going for a clean sweep."

Brognola hung up and Katz did, too.

"Uncle Saul sends his love," the Israeli told Phoenix Force.

"We always were a close family," James explained to Agent Fisher.

"So," McCarter asked, "what did dear old uncle have to say?"

"He called to let us know about a shipment of acetic anhydride that was due to arrive at Don Muang International about three hours ago."

"Acetic anhydride," Fisher repeated. "And a whole planeload of it's coming in?"

Katz nodded and held up a piece of paper he'd copied the information on. "I've got the particulars right here. Uncle Saul wasn't sure of the plane's ultimate destination, but if we can verify that it did land at Don Muang, maybe we can find out."

"This crap doesn't get any better, does it?" Fisher said. "Having that much acetic anhydride slip into Thailand can only spell trouble. The Thai government hasn't done too badly establishing a chemical-free zone in the country, but with whole planeloads of the stuff flying in under their noses, that pretty much tosses the chemical-free angle right out the window.''

Agent Fisher's alarm was understandable. That such a substantial amount of acetic anhydride had apparently been smuggled safely into Thailand clearly showed that an already miserable situation was growing worse. Acetic anyhydride was one of the precursor chemicals necessary for refining opium into heroin.

''If we're only several hours behind the shipment of the chemical,'' Manning said, ''then it shouldn't be too difficult to pick up its trail. Bringing it in by the planeful, though, sure sounds like a stunt the bunch we're looking for would pull.''

''And it ties in with what Sutha Nakhon told us,'' Encizo added, ''about putting the Golden Triangle's heroin production under one roof. Pulling off a scheme that grand would require an abundant supply of the precursor chemicals.''

''And if we can trace where the acetic anhydride winds up,'' James said, ''then maybe we can locate the four big shots we missed in Pattaya.''

Fisher said to Katz, ''Mind if I take a look at the information on that flight?''

Katz held out the paper. ''Be my guest.''

Agent Fisher took the sheet and, with Katzenelenbogen's permission, picked up the phone to place a few calls. He had a friend who knew somebody who worked at Don Muang International. The DEA man asked a few questions, then waited for callbacks.

McCarter, meanwhile, helped himself to another can of Coke from the fridge. A single phone call answered Fisher's inquiry, and he relayed the news to Phoenix Force.

"We've got them." Fisher smiled. "The flight was scheduled to land at Don Muang more than three hours ago, but there was a delay at Manila International, and the plane got into Don Muang ninety minutes late."

"Is it still at the airport?" Manning asked.

Fisher shook his head. "It stayed on the ground long enough to refuel, then took off again. Its reported destination was the airport an hour north of us in Chiang Mai."

"Excellent," Katz said. "Then it looks like we'll be heading that way ourselves."

"I don't imagine it would do me any good to ask to come along for the ride?" Fisher wondered.

"Sorry," Katz said. "We're really grateful for all you've done for us, but we have to tackle this problem on our own."

"Have any of you guys ever been to Chiang Mai?" Fisher asked, and when each of the Phoenix team members responded negatively, the DEA special agent did not appear surprised. "All right. I accept that you're not taking me with you to Chiang Mai, but at least let me give you the name of someone to contact once you arrive. He's dependable and he knows Chiang Mai. He could save you a lot of unnecessary aggravation."

"Your concern is appreciated, Fisher," Katz said. "But since the safety of the DEA has been compromised here in Bangkok, there's every likelihood that the same thing has happened in Chiang Mai."

"The man I'll put you in touch with isn't DEA," Fisher said. "He's a Thai Ranger I've personally worked twice with in the past."

"How good is he?" Katz asked, interested.

"He's not afraid to throw stones at the big boys, if that's what you mean," Fisher said. "And he's not one to lose his head in a firefight. If things get hairy like I think they stand a chance of doing, I can guarantee you won't regret having him by your side."

"What's this Thai Ranger's name?" Katz asked.

"Narong Poolsri," Fisher replied. "You'll be doing yourselves one hell of a favor if you contact him when you hit Chiang Mai—which also happens to be where Narong was born. What do you say?"

Katz looked at each of his men in turn, then said to Fisher, "Sold."

## 19

The man they had come to the bar in Chiang Mai to find was sitting alone at a table enjoying a beer and listening to music playing over a pair of speakers attached to the wall. He looked up as they approached, but said nothing, watching passively as the five strangers spread out and encircled his table.

"Narong Poolsri?" Katz inquired.

The Thai Ranger sipped his beer. He could have been anywhere between twenty-five and forty years old. His black hair was cropped short and he was dressed in a two-piece camouflage suit that accentuated his compact muscular frame.

He sipped again at his beer, then said, "Who wants to know?"

"A friend of yours from Bangkok advised us to look you up in Chiang Mai," Katz explained. "That is, if you are Narong Poolsri."

"Who is this friend in Bangkok?"

"Ralph Fisher."

"The name Fisher," the Thai said cautiously, "is not unfamiliar to me."

"You are Narong Poolsri, then?"

The man nodded.

"May we join you?" Katz asked.

"Are you offering to buy me a beer?"

Katz said yes, and Narong, curious, motioned for Phoenix Force to sit. "The hospitality of my table is yours."

"And about bleedin' time, too," McCarter said, pulling out a chair and taking the seat immediately to Narong's right. "That's better."

The rest of the Stony Man crew sat down at the table as Narong called out for six bottles of Singha lager.

"Cold Coca-Cola Classic for me, if you don't mind, mate," McCarter requested.

Narong amended the order and a couple of minutes later was raising his glass in a traditional Thai toast. *"Chai yo!"* he said.

"You got it," James added as he sampled his drink.

"Very good," Narong said, when half of his glass was drained. "Now that we have shared a drink together, perhaps you gentlemen could tell me why Agent Fisher suggested that you come to see me."

"Do you know of a Thai called Manas Roopka-chorn?" Katz questioned.

"The former wing commander and brother to Ma-noon Roopkachorn," Narong said. "Manas and Ma-noon attempted to overthrow the government some time ago. Manas is dead now. He had the presence of mind to get himself killed in Pattaya over the weekend."

"We know," Katz said. "We were there when Manas lost his life."

Narong's dark eyes widened slightly. "Most interesting. And how is it that five *farangs* traveled to Pattaya to assist such a traitor as Manas in leaving this world? I know by looking at you that you are not in the employ of the Royal Thai government."

"No, we are not," Katz confirmed. "We have been sent to Thailand by others. Are you aware of the deaths of the DEA special agents in Bangkok last week?"

"Yes," Narong said. "They were four of Fisher's associates."

Katz nodded. "Correct. Manas and his brother, Manoon, as well as three others, were responsible for the deaths. It is our job to see to it that such acts are not repeated."

"These 'others' you speak of. You know their names?"

"Lo Hsing Han, General Ma and Chang Chi-Fu— none of whom should be a stranger to you."

Puzzled, Narong drank more of his beer. "For Manas and Manoon to do business with those three is extraordinary. In times past each of the men you have named has been counted as the others' enemy. How is it that they have finally set aside their differences?"

"We have determined," Manning said, "that the five men entered into a partnership to consolidate all heroin production in Thailand under their control."

"With the resources at their disposal," Narong said, "such a union could be devastating. By working together and not fighting one another, they could increase the annual output of heroin dramatically. Already, the money coming in from selling the end-product of the opium poppy is great. Having more to sell would give them more to spend. Do you have any ideas what they could be interested in buying with that money?"

"Possibly," James offered, "that's where Manas and Manoon figured into the deal. Maybe the extra money would be used to finance another coup attempt."

"And with the Roopkachorn brothers in power—" Narong followed James's suggestion to its logical conclusion "—then Chang and the rest would have the blessing of the government to further increase their production and sale of heroin. What you gentlemen are telling me is a nightmare, one that could conceivably come true."

"I'm glad you feel that way," Katz said.

"How can I feel otherwise?" Narong asked. "The continued cultivation of opium—and its refinement into heroin—is a cruel rape of all that is decent. There are people, I know, who excuse the manufacture and distribution of heroin from within the Golden Triangle by saying that it would not exist if the addicts of Europe and the United States were not so demanding.

"This might be partially true, but such narrow-mindedness conveniently sweeps under the carpet the addiction problem in Burma, Thailand and Laos. In Thailand alone we have more than half a million addicts who are slaves night and day to the slow death of heroin.

"With a problem of this magnitude, I am blind to nationalities. We are one world, one people. What affects one country affects all countries. The disease of addiction infects all nations, and the only way to kill that disease is to go to its source. Manoon, Chang and the others must not be allowed to carry out their scheme. How can I help you?"

"We have reason to believe that the men we are seeking have established a sophisticated opium refinery somewhere in the vicinity of Chiang Mai," Katz said. "When we met up with Manas in Pattaya on Sunday, we fully expected to find his brother and their partners there also. Unfortunately, the others had departed before we arrived, leaving Manas on his own to prepare a welcome for us."

"They suspected you were coming to Pattaya, then." Narong smiled as though remembering something amusing. "The five of you wouldn't know anything about a ferocious gun battle that took place on the streets of Bangkok's Potpong district last Saturday night, would you?"

"Guilty as charged," Encizo answered. "We were there."

"And the gunfight earlier that day on the *khlongs* of the city," Narong ventured, "was that you, too?"

"We had a busy weekend," McCarter candidly revealed.

"So it would seem," Narong said. "What makes you think Manoon and the others fled to Chiang Mai?"

"At this point we don't know for certain they did," Katz admitted. "But what made us suspect they might be here was learning of a large shipment of acetic anhydride that was flown into Chiang Mai earlier today."

"One of the chemicals required in the refining process," Narong stated. "We have been trying to establish northern Thailand as a chemical-free zone for years now. How much acetic anhydride are we talking about?"

"An entire planeload," Katz told him, to which Narong whistled softly.

"Such a quantity would seem to indicate someone is planning to refine an enormous amount of opium into heroin," he said. "Still, it coincides with rumors that have been floating around Chiang Mai the past month or so. These rumors tell of a prominent Chinese chemist smuggled into Thailand under the protection of Chang's San United Amy."

"This Chinese chemist," Katz said, "is he believed to be staying in Chiang Mai?"

"Perhaps he was," Narong answered, "but no longer. My friends and I scoured the city in search of him without success. Undoubtedly, he did not wish to be found. He was wise, don't you think?"

"Any idea where the chemist disappeared to?" asked James.

"There are many possibilities," Narong said. "There are those who believe he was never here in the first place, but existed in imagination only. Myself, I think the chemist was definitely in Chiang Mai, and the reason we did not find him was that he was already working somewhere in the mountains to the north, performing whatever task it is Chang Chi-Fu hired him for.

"Now, with this information about the huge delivery of acetic anhydride today to Chiang Mai, I begin to make sense of the unseen Chinese chemist in Thailand."

"Would you suggest this chemist is here to oversee the production of heroin at the opium refinery my friends and I are searching for?" Katz proposed.

"I am sure of it," Narong said with conviction. "And locating the refinery might reveal more than a chemist and his chemicals. If Manoon, Lo Hsing Han, old General Ma and Chang are involved, it would not surprise me to find them with the chemist. But where is the refinery?"

"How difficult would it be to find out?" Katz questioned.

"Difficult, but not impossible," the Thai answered. "But only if you have someone with you who is just as much at home in the wild as he is in the city. Even *farangs* such as yourselves might find the refinery with a man like that by your side."

Colonel Katzenelenbogen laughed. "You know such a man?"

It was Narong's turn to laugh. "Intimately."

**20**

"You have done well, Li Hua," Chang said, congratulating the brilliant Chinese chemist he had personally recruited. "To have produced so much heroin in only four weeks truly represents a remarkable achievement."

Li Hua bowed slightly, acknowledging the compliment of his employer. "With the facilities you have so generously placed at my disposal, Chang Chi-Fu, it would be unjust for me to accept all the credit for our first month's output. Still, modesty aside, I humbly agree with your assessment of our success. The nearly eight metric tons we produced surpassed even my expectations."

"Then you feel you will not have trouble producing about the same amount during the second month?" Chang asked.

"No trouble whatsoever," Li Hua assured the former Burmese milita commander and present leader of the San United Army. "And with the safe arrival of the acetic anhydride, I think I would not be far wrong in supposing that our second month's production level will be greater than our first."

Chang seemed impressed. "Did you hear that, Manoon?" he called across the dining table to where the brooding Thai had sat for the past thirty minutes, staring vacantly at his plate. "Li Hua is already confident of increasing next month's production to more than eight metric tons! We are fortunate to have such a skilled associate."

"Yes," Manoon repeated absently. "Fortunate, indeed."

General Ma looked up with a frown, his spoon brimming with noodles and pork. "Enough of your moodiness, Manoon. I grow weary of your oppressive sorrow. For two days now you have worn the burden of your brother's death like a shroud. A good way to suffocate, if you ask me. Why can't you accept what happened to Manas and be done with it? I am sure he would not want you brooding over his death. He would want you celebrating the success of our partnership with the rest of us."

"It is interesting how well you understand my brother's desires now that he is dead," Manoon said. "Even more interesting when you consider that you knew him not at all when he was alive. As for my grief, General Ma, I am sorry if it displeases you. You might be willing to forget the sacrifice Manas made for us, but I am not. The celebration you would have me enjoy is tainted by my brother's blood."

"Nonsense," General Ma said, shoveling the noodles and pork into his mouth. "Pure nonsense. Every war has its casualties."

"Then my regret, General Ma," Manoon confessed, "is that this war did not claim an additional victim in Pattaya. But that would have been unlikely, no? You have not managed to live your many years by being the last into the lifeboat every time the ship goes down."

General Ma sputtered, choking on a piece of pork he soon washed down with some iced coffee. "You ineffectual excuse for a soldier! You dare to accuse me of cowardice?"

"I accuse you of nothing," Manoon replied innocently, pleased to have at last pierced General Ma's bubble of false pride. "Cowardice is, after all, such a dishonorable trait. Don't you agree?"

General Ma threw his spoon and fork to the table in a fit of anger. "This is an outrage. To be labeled a coward by one like yourself is unthinkable. Your implication that I would be the first to abandon a sinking ship is not appreciated. I demand an apology."

Manoon gave the impression of considering the demand, then said to General Ma, "Very well, I apologize."

Barely satisfied, General Ma mumbled and coughed, then said grudgingly as he resumed eating, "And I accept your apology."

"Yes," Manoon continued in all seriousness, "I see I was wrong to believe you would run for the lifeboat at the first indication of your ship's distress. I see now that, for a man like you, a lifeboat would be unnecessary."

General Ma frowned, a spoonful of noodles dangling in front of his mouth like an army of white worms. "That does not sound like an apology."

"My meaning is clear," Manoon said. "With all the fat stored in that corpulent backside of yours, I should be amazed if you *could* sink."

General Ma's face went red with rage. He dropped his fork and spoon and pushed away from the table as Lo Hsing Han, who sat next to him, intervened.

"There, there," counseled the Burmese Communist Party leader. "This is no time to be quarreling among ourselves. We are letting emotions stand in the path of reason, which is always a mistake. Manoon, you have worked hard so that the profits of our partnership would enable you to wrest the mantle of power from the Royal Thai government. The fact that Manas is no longer beside you to share the realization of that dream should not cause you to abandon your goals— not now when that dream is within your grasp.

"And you—" the BCP leader turned to General Ma like a teacher addressing an unruly student "—with your vast wealth of experience, General, should realize that Manoon's critical words came from his heart, and not from his head. We have all lost loved ones to the whims of violence, General Ma, yourself included. Can you not overlook statements that I am sure would never have been made but for the depth of Manoon's grief?''

Before General Ma could answer, Chang spoke up. ''Lo Hsing Han's remarks are most apt. Grief has clouded Manoon's judgment briefly, but with our support he will soon be himself again.''

Chang was content to be conciliatory for the time being, knowing as he did that he would soon be free from all the bickering and backbiting.

Chang believed his partners were deluded fools to think he would honor their so-called union of trust once their refinery here in the rugged mountains above Chiang Mai proved able to produce substantial amounts of heroin on a regular full-time basis. Who needed the constant headaches provided by deluded fools? Not Chang Chi-Fu!

General Ma would be the first to go. The pompous hothead would never learn to hold his temper in check. That temper would eventually endanger everything the partnership had worked so hard to achieve. Chang was sure Manoon would go along with any plans to eliminate General Ma permanently.

Manoon would be the next to die. Once General Ma was gone, Manoon would grow careless and lower his guard. When he was lulled into feeling comfortable and safe, Chang would strike his ignorant inferior down.

Last to go would be the gullible Lo Hsing Han. Blinded by the fact that he and Chang were both Burmese, Lo Hsing Han would never suspect Chang of plotting to kill him until it was too late. Long after Lo Hsing Han had breathed his last, Chang Chi-Fu would be reaping the rewards of his infinite patience.

"Well?" Chang asked Manoon and General Ma. "What do you say? Are we to be stalemated by your stubbornness, or may we proceed on course with our unified strength to guide us?"

General Ma stared long and hard at Manoon, his anger seeping out of him like hot air leaking from a balloon. He sat down again, then turned up the corners of his mouth in a strained semblance of a smile.

"I yield to your soothing words of wisdom, my friends," the aged commander of the KMT said to Chang and Lo Hsing Han. "Perhaps I have been a shade insensitive to Manoon's terrible loss. Not so long ago I lost my own brother in similar circumstances. I would do well to remember my feelings then so as to better understand Manoon's feelings now."

*"Mai pen rai,"* Manoon said. "It was unfair of me perhaps, to expect General Ma to understand the extent of my loss. What is shared between brothers can never be fully understood by outsiders. I see that now and accept it, and would ask General Ma to disregard any disrespect I might have shown toward his illustrious career, and to ignore, as well, any references made in anger to his physical appearance."

General Ma nodded curtly.

"Excellent," Chang said, doing his best not to sound like a referee who had just prevented a fight between two children on a playground. "I am pleased there is now no ill will to dampen our impending journey south to Khao Soon."

"Indeed," General Ma put in with enthusiasm, "we all look forward to the conclusion of this initial stage of our partnership. Once our first delivery of heroin has been made to Khao Soon, then forever more we may expect to reap the profits of our efforts." With nothing more appropriate readily available, he raised his glass of iced coffee in a toast. "May our partnership endure through the months and years ahead. May our friendship ever grow. And—" he nodded at Manoon "—may we never forget in our hearts the sacrifice made by Manas Roopkachorn. Long may his memory remain!"

With that General Ma drained the glass of iced coffee. The others joined the toast with their own beverages. Chang was the last to lower his glass. As he did so, the door of the dining room opened, and one of Chang's SUA men entered.

"Excuse me, Chang Chi-Fu," the armed man interrupted.

"Yes, what is it?" Chang requested with a flourish.

"I am to inform you that all of the product has been loaded onto the train, and that the honor guard is ready for you to board at your convenience."

"Splendid," Chang said. "You may tell Captain Direkarn that we will be out directly, as soon as we have finished our meal."

"Very well." The SUA man bowed, then turned and left them.

A quarter of an hour later Chang and his partners, along with the Chinese chemist, Li Hua, rose from the table and made their way outside. During dinner the fading yellow light that signaled the end of day in the mountainous countryside had all but given way to a spreading blanket of purple and black. Here and there the first twinkling stars of night could already be seen peeking through the treetops to the east.

The coming of darkness did not hamper operations in the opium refinery compound. Designed to function on a twenty-four-hour basis, the refinery was equipped with its own power generating station, to which were attached numerous floodlights mounted on tree trunks and metal support poles. When Chang and the others appeared, these floodlights had been switched on, and the area encompassing the refinery was bathed in artificial light.

When the refinery was built, not one tree in the forest had had to be cut down to make room for construction. The reason for this had nothing to do with conservation, however, but was simply practical: to make it difficult to spot the refinery from the air.

The complex comprised six buildings of varying sizes, laid out to form a large rectangle. They included two barracks, each capable of housing thirty men, a mess hall, a laboratory and a warehouse to store the heroin prior to shipping.

The sixth building was a single-story private residence, complete with all amenities, at the center of the compound. Chang and his associates lived there while visiting the refinery, and Li Hua's quarters were there, too.

The compound was not enclosed by a wall. Again the designers had elected to retain as much of the natural forest as possible.

With Chang Chi-Fu in the lead, the four surviving partners and Li Hua walked eagerly across the compound to the warehouse, which was immediately opposite the laboratory. At the rear of the warehouse railroad tracks linked the refinery to the outside world. On the tracks was a steam-powered locomotive, with eight cars and a caboose trailing behind, a great gray cloud rising from its smokestack.

Everyone working at the refinery had turned out to see the heroin-laden train depart on its maiden trip to the distribution center far to the south. Anticipation ran high. It was common knowledge that once the run between the refinery and Khao Soon was established, all the participants responsible for the refinery's success would profit handsomely.

Captain Direkarn was standing at attention as Chang Chi-Fu approached.

"We are ready when you are, Chang Chi-Fu," the captain reported, saluting smartly. "The cargo is safely stored in the boxcars, and the men we are taking south with us are also on board. We await your word to depart.''

Chang returned his captain's salute, then said, ''Very well, Captain Direkarn. We are as anxious to leave as you are.'' The SUA leader turned to Li Hua. ''Work hard in our absence, my friend, for when we return these boxcars will be empty.''

''Have no fear,'' Li Hua responded with authority. ''My assistants and I are prepared to work tirelessly. Give us empty boxcars and we will fill them again and again.'' He bowed formally. ''A safe journey and a swift ride home.''

Then Li Hua stood aside as Captain Direkarn spun on his heel and led Chang, Manoon Roopkachorn, Lo Hsing Han and old General Ma aboard the train.

## 21

Concealed within the forest of teak and pine trees, Phoenix Force and their Thai guide, Narong, watched from a distance as the train loaded with heroin slowly pulled away from the refinery warehouse. Of the six men, only McCarter viewed it with an expression of pure frustration on his face.

"Stuff it!" the cockney protested quietly, confident that the departing train would cover the sound of his words. "The four geezers we expected to find in Pattaya with Manas are getting away!"

"It is prudent to let them leave this time," Narong advised. "First things first... Isn't that the expression?"

"It is and you're right," Katz told the Thai. "By letting the train depart without interference, we are roughly cutting by half the number of troops left to defend the refinery." The Israeli commando passed the binoculars to Narong. "Your count was accurate, Narong. Besides the four enemy leaders and the engineer and his assistant, an additional twenty to twenty-five men are passengers on the train. The same num-

ber of armed men have remained behind at the refinery.''

"Including the Chinese chemist," Narong said.
"He was the one bowing to Chang just before the train
pulled out. I cannot wait to get my hands around his
scrawny neck. Before the night is over I want the
pleasure of squeezing his life from his body.''

"All that's fine, mate," McCarter said, "but what
about the bleedin' train?" He pointed as the caboose
rounded a bend in the tracks and vanished. "If we let
the train go now we might lose it for good.''

"That is unlikely," Narong assured McCarter. "I
know the mountains above Chiang Mai as well as I
know Chiang Mai itself. The train can take only one
route, and the trip down the mountains, with many
sharp curves and in the darkness of night, is a slow
one. It will buy us the time we need to complete our
work here before going after the train.''

"We did see the last of the heroin being loaded onto
the train," James recalled. "It's a cinch they're not
going to transport it farther north. The real money for
a delivery of this magnitude lies somewhere to the
south.''

"In the direction of Bangkok, or possibly farther
south than that," Narong confirmed. "Which is why
I am not alarmed to see the train disappear. Having
once seen it, I will be able to find the train for us again.
You have my word on it—" he glanced at McCarter
then added "—mate.''

Finding the hidden opium refinery had not been easy for Phoenix Force. After leaving the bar where they had shared a drink with Narong, the five men proceeded with their guide to one of Chiang Mai's many *wats*, or temples, so that Narong could pray and receive a blessing from the Buddhist monks.

"Thank you for waiting," Narong said as he emerged from the temple. "It may be difficult for Westerners to comprehend, but I always feel more ready to begin a new project after I have paid my respects to Buddha."

"A man's religion is his personal business," Katz assured the Thai. "Where do we go now?"

"Hunting," Narong replied.

Beginning at the airport where the plane bearing the load of acetic anhydride had arrived in Chiang Mai, Narong and Phoenix Force played detectives for the rest of the day. No one at the airport knew anything helpful. Even memory enhancers of crisp currency failed to provide any useful leads. The plane had landed, its cargo had been removed and the plane had taken off again. What had become of the cargo or those who picked it up was anybody's guess.

Returning empty-handed to Chiang Mai, they stopped for a late lunch at a roadside chicken stew restaurant where Narong ordered a delicious meal that did not require a fire hydrant to wash it down. As they ate, Narong summed up their chances of tracking down the acetic anhydride.

"It doesn't look good," he said. "With everyone at the airport playing dumb about who picked up the shipment, the trail might have grown too cold by now for us to follow it to the refinery."

Sensing from Narong's tone that he was ready to tackle the problem from another direction, Katz asked, "What would you suggest, then?"

"Suppose the refinery is in the mountains above Chiang Mai as you say," the Thai began. "Producing vast quantities of heroin would be an exercise in futility without the means to transport that heroin to market."

"Of course," Manning put in. "For people to carry that much heroin would be impractical. What's the alternative?"

"Chang and his partners could be using elephants for the job," Narong suggested.

"Elephants?" James raised an eyebrow.

"Certainly," Narong said. "Unlike many countries where elephants are merely circus performers, in Thailand we take the great gray beasts of burden much more seriously. My country's lumber industry relies heavily on hardworking elephants to drag the felled trees down from the mountains."

"Well," said Katz, "it may be feasible for elephants to transport the heroin, but I doubt such a method would be suitable to the needs of our adversaries, for two reasons. First, elephants would be slow. In any business time is money—this one is no different. The longer it takes Chang and his friends to get the heroin into the hands of buyers, the longer it takes for them to get paid for their product.

"The second reason I rule out elephants concerns security. The heroin would be extremely vulnerble to attack from hostile forces, either competitors or representatives of the Royal Thai government."

"There is logic to what you say," Narong told the Israeli. "So if we exclude elephants, then the only other possibility I see would be for Chang and his partners to bring the heroin out by rail."

When they finished their meal they proceeded to the Thai Ministry of Transportation office in Chiang Mai, where they pored over detailed maps of the region's railway system. Half an hour into the latest leg of their investigation, McCarter noted something unusual.

"That's odd," the Briton said, tracing his finger along the route of a set of tracks climbing into the mountains. "I can see where these tracks start, and I can see where they lead to, but I can't make out where these tracks branching off them go."

"Let me find out." Narong swept the map into his arms and hurried to discuss the matter with the managing director of the transportation office. Minutes later he returned with the information. "I believe this is the break we have been searching for."

"You discovered where the offshoot of track leads?" Encizo asked.

Narong nodded. "According the files in this office, those tracks go nowhere. Their construction was commissioned more than a year ago by a group of

Bangkok businessmen who planned to put up an unspecified number of buildings about six miles off the main railroad line."

"Buildings for what purpose?" James asked.

"Apparently for some exclusive mountain retreat for wealthy Thais and foreigners," Narong explained. "The six miles of track were laid but—and this is what makes me suspicious—shortly afterward the Bangkok businessmen funding the project experienced a series of financial setbacks, and the project was never completed."

"But the six miles of tracks remain?" Katz, like the others, sensed they had found what they were looking for.

"Yes," Narong answered. "Abandoned and unused."

"Yeah, well, let's go see for ourselves!" McCarter said, leaping to his feet.

For security's sake, Katz instructed Narong to drive them as far as he could up the side of the mountain opposite to where the exclusive retreat was to have been built. Following the railway tracks for a frontal approach to the site would have been much faster, but not necessarily as healthy. The enemy's resources in manpower could not be ignored. Better to sacrifice a little time, everyone agreed, than walk into a situation from which there was no exit.

The wisdom of approaching the site from the back became evident long before they reached their goal.

The wind blowing in their direction carried a faintly familiar odor.

"You guys smell that?" Manning asked in a whisper.

McCarter tested the air. "Reminds me of vinegar."

"More like acetic anhydride," Katz said. "I think we've found ourselves an opium refinery."

The sun was sinking slowly in the west when Phoenix Force and Narong arrived at their destination. The six men watched in silence as the last of the boxcars was loaded with heroin, and Chang and the others boarded the train.

Now, with the noise of the train's departure fading in the distance, McCarter was more eager than ever to launch their strike against the refinery.

"We'll let the train get farther down the mountain before we make our move," Katz counseled. Then he outlined his plan for the coming attack.

## 22

Moving as one with the night, the shadow reached the laboratory of the refinery unseen. When he was certain his movements had not been detected, Manning pulled a black ditty bag off his shoulder and went to work.

Confident that the refinery's remote location rendered it inaccessible, the enemy had turned off the floodlights illuminating the compound soon after the departure of the train an hour before. Nor were there any guards patrolling the area. Everyone in the camp, with the exception of the Chinese chemist, was in the mess hall eating dinner. Through the mess hall doors Manning could hear tinny music from a radio.

Working noiselessly with the speed of a professional, Manning removed ten ounces of C-4 plastic explosive and affixed the white puttylike substance under an exhaust vent at the rear of the laboratory where the fumes of acetic anhydride were strongest. The quantity of explosive was more than enough for what Manning had in mind, but the extra C-4 would not go to waste. He wanted an attention grabber for the initial explosion. With ten ounces of C-4 he was sure to get his wish.

The explosive securely in place, the demolition expert inserted a pencil detonator and set its timer for five minutes. Then he slung the ditty bag over his shoulder again and crossed to the warehouse where he quickly applied another ten-ounce block of C-4 to the outer edge of the door. He set the timer for this deposit of explosive for eight minutes, then again shouldered his bag and melted into the darkness.

Two minutes later Manning was back where he'd started from, beside a small stream whose water was used by the laboratory in the process of refining opium into morphine, and then refining morphine further still into heroin. Rafael Encizo was waiting for him.

The Cuban handed over the H&K G3 SG1 sniper rifle he had been covering Manning with, and whispered softly, "When's show time?"

Manning answered by holding up two fingers, then brought the NOD scope attached to the H&K rifle to his eye. The NOD device could take any available light, such as that from the moon or stars, and amplify it up to sixty thousand times. Viewed through the scope, the refinery compound appeared on the scanner as though on a miniature television screen.

Manning moved the scope slowly as he scanned from one end of the camp to the other. He stopped momentarily at the front porch of the private residence when he saw the Chinese chemist outside, apparently for a breath of fresh air. The rest of the men at the compound were still gathered in the mess hall.

As Manning completed his recon he spotted McCarter and James, then Katzenelenbogen and Narong Poolsri. James and McCarter were near one of the barracks, while the Israeli colonel and the Thai were entrenched behind a dense clump of teakwood trees at the far end of the compound, directly opposite the laboratory and warehouse.

It was time to take cover. Manning lowered his weapon and ducked behind a tree trunk, and Encizo did the same. Then the detonator triggered the first block of C-4 and transformed the refinery into a living hell. A technicolor rush of rumbling noise and destruction filled the night and seemed to stretch on forever.

Fed by the fury of the explosion, the fumes of acetic anhydride discharged by the laboratory's exhaust vent ignited in a mighty secondary blast that roared through the building and reduced it to a flaming inferno. Fire splashed the darkness with orange-red light and pelted the ground with burning raindrops.

The first wave of enemy gunmen spilled from the mess hall, their automatic weapons drawn and ready. A few had not managed to grab their weapons in their haste to escape the fiery Hades inside the building. These men ran empty-handed, more concerned with survival than with combating saboteurs.

Phoenix Force held its fire and gave its opponents plenty of time to get out of the mess hall and investigate the twin eruptions. Katz's plan of attack called for deceiving their foes into thinking some mishap in the laboratory had caused the explosions. The plan was working beautifully.

One SUA gunman gesticulated wildly and shouted orders to the rest of the soldiers under his command. Instantly, four of his men broke away from the crowd and rushed in the direction of the warehouse. Four more SUA spun on their heels and charged toward the barracks. The heat from the blazing ruins of the lab washed over everyone else.

As the SUA gunmen ran straight toward him and James, McCarter wielded his Ingram. Both it and James's Smith & Wesson M-76 were equipped with foot-long sound suppressors. Three of the SUA hoodlums were armed, but the fourth had failed to grab a weapon.

The Phoenix Force duo concentrated on the three armed men. Two killers bowed out of the fight, their chests ventilated by 9 mm parabellums, courtesy of McCarter's M-10. James's weapon eliminated another SUA goon.

The unarmed fourth man surprised the two Phoenix Force fighters. Instead of bolting for cover or raising his hands in surrender, the guy kept coming. He leaped toward Calvin James, one leg extended in a desperate flying jump kick. The tactic was so outrageous, it worked. His foot slammed into James's M-76, kicking the S&W subgun from the black man's grasp.

The Thai kick-boxing expert landed nimbly on one foot, pivoted and thrust a kick to James's midsection. The black warrior doubled up and the SUA hood whipped a backfist to James's face. The warrior fell. The Thai shouted a war whoop as he leaped in the air and prepared to stamp both feet on the fallen American's chest.

McCarter held his fire, fearful of hitting James. The black man rolled to avoid the murderous stomp. His opponents's feet slammed into the ground next to him. The Phoenix fighter from Chicago lashed out with a kick to the man's kidney, pitching the Thai head over heels. James scrambled to his feet as the other man got up, too.

James assumed a tae kwon-do T-stance while his opponent adopted a kick-boxer's on-guard position, fists balled, weight balanced on the balls of his feet. The thug attacked, snapping a kick at James's groin, then jerked back his foot. The battle-wise karate expert realized his Thai opponent's kick was a feint. He jumped back to avoid the real attack, a whirling roundhouse kick, aimed for his head.

James slammed a snap kick to his opponent's side, his steel-toed paratrooper boot striking the man under the ribs. The Thai groaned, but retaliated immediately with a flying knee-kick aimed at James's chest.

The black warrior dodged the attack and jabbed his left fist at his opponent's face.

Then an elbow smashed into James's forearm. Pain vibrated up his arm to his shoulder as the Thai launched a punch at his face. The Phoenix fighter blocked the punch with his right forearm to the inside of his opponent's wrist. Both men thrust right-fist strokes simultaneously. The Thai's punch was deflected by the palm of James's left hand. The black warrior's knuckles crashed into his opponent's nose. Blood spurted from the man's nostrils as he staggered backward.

James suddenly jumped forward and unleashed a flying side kick. His boot slammed under the Thai's jaw. The powerhouse kick thrust the man's head back so forcibly that vertebrae snapped like toothpicks in a steel vise. The Thai fell heavily, his neck broken.

A gunman standing next to the SUA commander saw the four men die, and pointed excitedly in the direction of the fallen bodies. Lit by the crackling flames of the ravaged laboratory, his face was a mask of surprise-shaded fear. He realized now that the explosions and resulting fire had been deliberately set, and screamed for his men to take cover.

Knowing their chances of reaching the barracks safely were virtually nil, many of the Thai, Burmese and Chinese gunmen tried to retreat into the mess hall, firing their weapons indiscriminately at an enemy they could not see.

Two of the fastest runners hit the lower steps of the mess hall porch as Rafael Encizo put his MP-5 machine pistol through its paces. The fleet-of-foot SUA killers were buried in a storm of 9 mm annihilation when the Cuban's H&K blaster let loose. As the H&K rounds impacted on their flesh, the hapless pair jerked and twitched on invisible wires, then slumped in a lifeless heap to the refinery's dirt floor.

A third SUA gunman suddenly charged, a Taiwanese Type-37 submachine gun in his fists. He pointed the Nationalist Chinese version of the American greasegun at Encizo and squeezed the trigger. The Cuban's reflexes responded automatically to the threat and he hurled himself sideways to the ground. Half a dozen 9 mm rounds sizzled above him as he aimed his MP-5 and squeezed off a 3-round burst. The Phoenix warrior's parabellums burned through the gunman's chest, ripping heart and lungs as the impact hurled him backward five feet.

When they saw their three comrades slain before their eyes, the half dozen SUA gunmen running behind them bolted in panic and rushed toward the only section of the refinery that seemed not to pose a threat. But their flight of terror brought them face-to-face with Katz's Uzi and Narong's home-grown Thai RPS-001 assault rifle.

Firing in unison, the Israeli commando and his Thai counterpart made short work of the fleeing SUA. Two of the Israeli's targets died, nursing nasty head wounds. A third gunman purchased his ticket to eternity with a trio of Uzi rounds that diced his internal organs to grisly confetti.

Patterned after the best the M-16 and AK-47 had to offer, Narong's RPS Thai assault rifle dispatched two of his adversaries with all the ease of a sledgehammer striking eggshells. Narong's RPS had a 30-round magazine, one-third of which took up residence in the unresisting flesh of the SUA gunmen the Thai brought down. Neither of Narong's targets lived long enough to realize they had been hit more than once.

The last opponent was unarmed. He had remained at the rear of the group that absorbed the wave of high-velocity destruction. Although terrified, he realized there was nowhere to run. The Thai hood grabbed the sagging body of one of his dead comrades and suddenly thrust the corpse at Narong. Literally a deadweight, it struck the Thai Ranger and knocked the RPS-001 rifle from his hands.

With a battle cry, the Thai thug charged forward and delivered a powerful side kick to Narong's chest. The Ranger was bowled over by the blow, but rolled on his neck and shoulders, kicking his legs overhead. He landed on one knee, arms raised defensively.

The SUA goon threw a kick at Narong's head, but the Ranger blocked with his forearms in an X position. Then he rose swiftly, picking up his opponent's leg in the process to throw him off balance. But the SUA thug had been well-schooled in Thai kick-boxing.

He did not resist when he started to fall, but he also caught the ground with one hand and used it to brace himself as he lashed out with his other foot.

The kick caught Narong in the ribs. He groaned and fell to one knee while the hoodlum hit the ground in a deft shoulder roll. Both men jumped to their feet. Katz aimed his Uzi at the SUA flunky, but did not fire because Narong was too close.

The Thai Ranger and the SUA thug squared off. Narong feinted a snap kick. The hood tried to block it and dropped his guard. Narong hit him in the side of the face with a right cross and followed with a flying knee kick to the midsection. The thug gasped from the blow, and Narong promptly butted his forehead into the bridge of his opponent's nose.

Narong stayed on his adversary. His fist tagged the man on the jaw. The stunned SUA creep staggered backward. The Ranger whirled, pivoting on one foot to lash the back of the other heel into his opponent's groin. The man doubled up with a choking groan. Narong jumped into the air, an arm raised overhead. He bent it at the elbow and brought it crashing down on the hoodlum's nape. The blow crushed a vertebra, breaking his neck and snapping the spinal cord simultaneously.

With the Starlite scope disengaged, Gary Manning raised his noise-suppressed H&K SG-1 sniper rifle to his shoulder and aimed at a clump of SUA troopers still clinging like frightened children to their commander's side as though he were the only hope for their salvation. With a deadly efficiency Manning proved their theory was incorrect.

Firing in a tightly packed left-to-right pattern, the Canadian sharpshooter emptied half of the G3's 20-round magazine into his mortally vulnerable opponents. Three SUA killers immediately paid with their lives for Manning's unerring accuracy with the big-bore battle rifle. Leaking from wounds in all the wrong places, the doomed SUA appeared to dance to music only they could hear, before they fell together in a cold dead heap.

Another Thai thug dropped to one knee and pointed his subgun in Manning's direction, but the Canadian marksman nailed him between the eyes with a 7.62 mm slug that killed him instantly.

Panicked into flight, another SUA goon bolted and tried to run to cover—somewhere, anywhere. Manning tracked him with the H&K rifle and pumped a bullet through his rib cage. The high-velocity round burned into the man's chest cavity, rearranging heart and lungs into useless mush. He was already half dead when he started to fall, but Manning fired another 7.62 mm slug into the side of his skull that completed the cycle that had begun the moment Phoenix Force chose its target.

Four SUA gunmen thanked whatever gods had inspired their commander to order them to secure the warehouse. When their friends started getting slaughtered like animals, they thought they were lucky to have escaped the worst of the attack.

Then the second deposit of C-5 Manning had planted suddenly exploded. Clustered too near the source of the explosion at the warehouse doors, the four gunmen were practically vaporized in a searing burst of heat and energy. A blinding light stabbed into their eyes.... Then they knew nothing.

The SUA commander and the last two of his men still alive died beneath a shower of flying debris from the destroyed warehouse. One SUA clawed frantically at a splinter of wood stuck in his neck. He gurgled and spit blood as he yanked the jagged splinter free, allowing even more blood to gush till he bled to death.

The gunman next to him fared no better, perishing with a gasp of finality after his eyes were pierced by a swarm of fiery toothpicks. He screamed and covered his face with his hands, blood streaming between his splayed fingers, and collapsed to his knees a heartbeat before he died.

Standing alone, encircled by the bodies of his troops, the dazed SUA commander seemed unaware at first that the right leg of his trousers had caught fire. Then the flames rippled over his uniform and turned him into a human torch. Arms flailing, the SUA officer discarded his submachine gun and began to dance around like one of those trick birthday candles that never blow out. His anguished screams shrilled through the air until Manning put him out of his misery with a solo G3 round through the back of his skull. As the screams abruptly died, so did the charred creature voicing them and the dead man's body flopped to the ground in a smoldering lump.

Phoenix Force and Narong waited a minute or so to see if any more SUA were waiting in the wings, but it soon became clear that the decisive attack had eliminated the enemy gunmen. One by one the members of the Stony Man crew and Narong emerged to survey the damage wrought by the explosions, the flames and their bullets.

"Everyone okay?" Katz asked, satisfied to note that, to a man, they had pulled through the encounter unscathed.

McCarter glanced at the carnage in the devastated compound. "That the lot of 'em, then?"

"Almost," said Narong.

When the initial C-4 load exploded outside the laboratory, the Chinese chemist taking the air on the porch of the residence quarters had quickly retreated to the safety of his building. Narong had seen him disappear and suspected he was still hiding somewhere inside.

"I will be right back," the Thai Ranger advised, then crossed to the residence and entered. Less than sixty seconds later he emerged with the chemist as his prisoner. "So, what do you think of my catch?"

"Well done," James answered for the rest of his team.

"I found the dog quivering behind the shower curtain of all things," Narong told them. "As you may guess, he was not overly pleased to see me." The Thai Ranger nudged the barrel of his RPS assault rifle into the chemist's back. "What is your name, dog?"

The chemist's face burned with anger and shame. "My name is Li Hua," he responded in halting English. "And I will tell you nothing."

"Noble," Narong pronounced, "but unacceptable." He dug the barrel of his rifle deeper into Li Hua's side. "We have no time to waste with the likes of you. Unless you answer our questions faithfully, you have my word I will personally cut out your tongue with a very dull knife, and then seal your mouth closed so you either choke to death or drown in your blood." He jabbed the chemist again with his rifle. "Well, what is to be?"

Li Hua's voice trembled, "Surely, you do not expect me to take your threats seriously. Making war with the others I can understand. They were armed and would have killed you had they had the chance. But me? I represent no danger to you. I am not your enemy. I have no weapon."

"Liar!" Narong accused. "Your skills as a chemist do more harm than all of these slain SUA put together. You are a murderer of infants, children, women and men. Because of you, lives are ruined and families are destroyed. But I grow weary of cataloging your sins. Prepare to die, dog known as Li Hua. Your time has come."

Narong slung his rifle over his shoulder and removed a knife from the sheath at his belt. Then he nodded to Manning and James. "While I pry out his tongue you must hold the dog still for me," he requested. "I expect he will struggle once the knife fills his mouth."

Manning and James grasped Li Hua firmly by the shoulders as Narong raised his knife and stepped forward.

"No, wait!" Li Hua cried, his resolve to stay silent wavering and then vanishing altogether at the sight of the Thai's blade.

"Open your mouth," Narong ordered, "or you will force me to carve my way in."

"No, no!" The Chinese chemist fought in vain to break free of the hold Manning and James had on him. "Put away your knife. There is no cause to mutilate me. I . . . I will answer your questions as you ask them."

"Very well," Narong said, "but I warn you. Let me once suspect you are lying, and having your tongue cut from your mouth will be the least of your worries. Do we understand each other?"

Li Hua hung his head and nodded.

"Good," Narong said, then turned to Katz. "I believe you would like a word with this dog?"

"Thank you," Katz said, squaring off in front of the completely demoralized Li Hua. "The train that left earlier with Chang Chi-Fu and the others on board . . . where are they taking the heroin?"

"Far to the south," Li Hua answered, watching the knife in Narong's hand from the corner of his eye. "Chang has established a secret distribution center where the heroin will be stored until it is sent to his European and American customers."

"And where is this distribution center located?" Katz demanded.

Li Hua gulped. "I have never been there."

"The bastard is lying." Narong slashed the air in front of Li Hua's face viciously with his knife. "At least give me the pleasure of cutting off his nose."

"No!" the chemist protested, his knees growing weak so that Manning and James had to support his weight. "What I tell you is true. I have never been to the distribution center. All I know is that it is somewhere in the south of Thailand."

"You'll have to be more specific, I'm afraid," Katz confessed, "or else I'm turning you over to my friend with the knife. The distribution center is in a city?"

"No," Li Hua replied. "It is to be found in a place called Khao Soon. That is all I know about it, I swear."

The Israeli looked to Narong. "Khao Soon? Do you know of such a place?"

"Yes," Narong said. "In English the name means Slaughter Mountain. Tungsten is mined there. There has been trouble there in the past, with gangs of poachers violating legitimate claims, but the turmoil is not as great today as it once was. Khao Soon would serve Chang and the others as an excellent location for their heroin distribution center."

"What is to become of me?" Li Hua timidly inquired. "Am I to be set free?"

Narong laughed harshly. "What? Let you go? So you can hire yourself out to the next Chang Chi-Fu who comes along to pay you to murder thousands from the comfort of your laboratory? Never! I would see you dead and rotting first."

"But," the chemist pleaded, "I answered your questions. I told you about Khao Soon."

"Which is the only reason I hesitate to kill you outright," Narong said. "We cannot take you with us. You will be lashed to a tree to await the arrival of the authorities we will send from Chiang Mai."

"What of the beasts of the forest?" Li Hua asked. "If you tie me to a tree, I will be unable to defend myself from a hungry animal."

"Then you had better pray the forest dwellers have dined elsewhere tonight, or that the men from Chiang Mai find you first," Narong advised. "I really do not care. I am letting you live for now, which is more than can be said for those you addict to the poison you create."

And without further discussion Narong tied the Chinese chemist to a tree, arms bound behind him so that escape was impossible and fixed a gag in his mouth.

"I am ready," Narong announced. "Shall we go?"

"Good idea, mate," McCarter agreed. "We've got a train to catch."

**23**

Chatree Udomwasana thought he was seeing things.

Riding in the watchtower of the caboose since the train had left the opium refinery many hours before, it was all the bored Chatree could do to keep awake. Camping in the crow's nest all night was a thankless job, made even worse by the monotonous clickety-click clickety-clack of the wheels upon the tracks that alternately conspired to drive him insane or put him to sleep. Orders were orders, however, and until old Aroon relieved him at daybreak, here in the caboose's cupola he would stay.

Dawn was already brightening the eastern skies, and Chatree was on the verge of dozing off again when the train slowed and moved into a tight curve. Sheer walls of rock bordered the tracks on each side. Chatree could see the silhouette of a footbridge up ahead, joining one craggy rock wall to the other. It seemed barely high enough to allow the smokestack of their train to pass beneath it.

Chatree had just recognized the footbridge when his eyes began playing tricks. No sooner had the smokestack cleared the bridge than he thought he saw not one, but four figures dressed in black hurl themselves off the bridge and onto the top of the boxcar below.

He was still trying to solve the mystery when a pair of muted thumps sounded on the caboose directly over his head. Momentarily distracted by the noise, he glanced away. By the time he looked back to where he imagined the four black-clad figures had landed, they were gone.

"You really must be dreaming," Chatree muttered to himself. "As soon as Aroon comes to relieve me, I am going straight to sleep."

"Psst!"

Chatree glanced down into the caboose and felt a bolt of icy fear stab him through the heart. Staring up at him were two apparitions out of a nightmare—both with dull black faces and eyes that glowed in the early-morning darkness inside the caboose. Most terrifying of all, Chatree noted in a flash of comprehension, these nightmares were carrying guns.

Dreaming or not, Chatree's hands streaked for the shotgun braced across his lap in a desperate bid to see if ghosts could be made to bleed. His fingers wrapped around the firearm just as the guns the nightmares carried coughed together and sent a chain reaction of agony bursting across his chest.

"He gets a minus two for speed," McCarter said, rating the dead man's performance.

"Like molasses," Manning said.

"If they're all like this bundle of lightning," the cockney concluded, "then we're home free."

Somewhere between the caboose and the locomotive the unmistakable chatter of a submachine gun rose above the noise of the steel wheels rolling on the tracks.

"Then again..." Manning said as he and McCarter hurried from the caboose.

"I know, I know," complained the Briton. "I could be wrong."

CALVIN JAMES LEAPED from the bridge a second ahead of Katz, Encizo and Narong. Feeling like a train robber out of America's wild and woolly West, the commando from Chicago landed on the boxcar, felt himself start to lose his balance, then recovered it again.

James looked over his shoulder to make sure the others had touched down safely as well. Reassured, he moved along the middle of the swaying boxcar in the direction of the caboose. Katz was right behind him. Narong and Encizo went the opposite way to deal with the engineer.

James reached the end of the boxcar and without hesitating jumped to the next one. It, too, was packed with processed heroin from the opium refinery in the mountains.

James and Katz made their way toward the third car, which was filled with passengers, the SUA gunmen accompanying Chang Chi-Fu and his partners south.

As James knelt and leaned out over the edge of the boxcar the train unexpectedly lurched to the left, throwing him back and then forward while he compensated for the abrupt shift of his weight. For a fraction of a second his head hung between the two cars.

For Surin Manechai, enjoying a cigarette while standing guard, the sight of James looking down at him was such a shock that the trigger-happy Thai whipped the business end of his submachine gun into the air and began blasting away.

James dived for cover as lead hornets gouged nasty holes through the roof of the boxcar near his feet, causing his toes to curl involuntarily in his boots. He reached for an M-26 grenade, pulled the pin while holding down the safety lever, then tossed the hand-held bomb over the side of the boxcar onto the platform where the SUA subgunner stood. James heard part of a frightened shriek before the M-26 exploded. Immediately, he was back on his feet and jumping to the passenger car filled with enemy troops.

When the first sounds of trouble filtered into the locomotive's cab, the train engineer turned in confusion to see if his assistant had an explanation. His question remained unasked. At that precise moment two black-clad gunmen scrambled over the top of the coal tender in the direction of the cab. The engineer's eyes registered shock as he whirled to reach for a rifle he kept handy hanging from a hook.

With a triple burst of 9 mm persuaders, Encizo's MP-5 put the engineer's efforts to arm himself on eternal hold. The engineer grunted loudly as the bullets pierced his side, causing him to arch his back and lose his balance.

The man screamed and started to fall. His assistant clutched at him madly, trying to save him, but gravity won in the end. The engineer tumbled headfirst from the cab, striking the wall of rock outside the train, then bouncing back and down, beneath the powerful wheels of the locomotive.

The assistant eyed his late friend's rifle. But the engineer's screams still echoed in his ears, and before he pulled himself together to grab the rifle, Narong and Encizo hopped into the cab.

"Good," Narong told the man in Thai. "I see you want to live."

The assistant engineer held up his hands in surrender. "What do you want me to do?"

"WHAT IS IT?" General Ma demanded, throwing open the door to his sleeping compartment and charging into the narrow corridor just outside. "Where is the shooting coming from?"

Manoon Roopkachorn, whose private compartment was in the same luxury coach, could only shake his head. "How should I know? It sounds like we are being attacked."

Then the grenade James had thrown exploded and General Ma gasped in surprise. "Of course, we are being attacked, you idiot! And you know damn good and well who it is, too—the infernal Americans your cowardly ass of a brother failed to kill for us in Pattaya!"

"I am pleased to hear you say that, General Ma," Manoon announced, producing a handgun from the pocket of his coat, and pointing it straight at General Ma's chest. "If it is the Americans, then I am not afraid. We outnumber them more than five to one. In a manner of speaking they have saved me the bother of having to kill you later. I can shoot you now, and blame your death on them."

General Ma looked at the gun in Manoon's hand and forced himself to laugh. "You are mad, Manoon."

"And you, General Ma, are dead."

The general lunged and Manoon fired, the single shot filling the corridor of their car with noise and gunsmoke. General Ma shouted and clamped his hand over the tiny hole in his shirt, feeling blood spurt from the wound each time his heart beat. The dying leader of the Chinese Irregular Forces managed to swat at Manoon with his free hand, then his knees collapsed under him. His face drained of all color and he breathed his last.

"I was curious how long it would take you to get around to that," Chang Chi-Fu said from behind.

Manoon turned with a start and made a feeble attempt to hide his handgun in his pocket. Chang was standing at the door leading into the car.

"How long have you been here?" Manoon asked.

"Long enough," Chang said. "Why did you do it?"

"It seemed a good idea at the time," Manoon said, pausing as more gunfire and exploding grenades came from the front of the train. "General Ma thought it was the Americans attacking us."

Chang nodded. "The late general was not a fool. I believe he was right."

Manoon eyed Chang suspiciously. "Where is Lo Hsing Han?"

"Where else?" Chang shrugged. "He is keeping General Ma company."

"You killed him?"

"You killed General Ma."

"That is different. The general was a dangerous man. I had to kill him. I had no choice."

"Neither have I," Chang insisted.

Before Manoon could stop him Chang whipped out a handgun of his own and put a bullet through the center of Manoon's forehead. The Thai's eyes rolled to the ceiling, then he fell to the floor and died.

"Neither have I," Chang repeated to the corpse of his former partner.

Then Chang returned to his own car to await the outcome of the fight.

Calvin James had almost reached the end of the roof of the passenger car he was rushing across when some of the SUA soldiers inside and below had the bright idea of shooting at the sound of the footsteps running overhead. The shots chased after the black commando's heels like a swarm of lead-lined bees lonesome for their hive, and their accuracy was too close for comfort.

Yakov Katzenelenbogen understood Calvin's dilemma and decided to give the SUA in the passenger car something else to think about. Letting his Uzi hang free by its lanyard, the Phoenix team's unit commander poked his left hand into his utility pouch and brought out a M-34 white phosphorus grenade.

He pulled the safety pin, then heaved the M-34 down through the hole made earlier by James's grenade. Cries of alarm greeted the M-34's arrival and then its detonator exploded, rupturing its body and exposing the WP.

Igniting on contact with air, the white phosphorous in the M-34 could burn for a minute at temperatures approaching 5,000 degrees Fahrenheit, a sobering piece of information more than a dozen SUA gunmen found out the hard way. White phosphorus ignited anything flammable, and the soldiers shooting at James were no exception.

As the fire swept through the passenger car, the SUA soldiers were engulfed by the all-consuming blaze that devoured flesh, burned through bones and melted eyeballs. The fortunate ones died instantly. Those who did not finished their miserable lives in agony, screaming until their throats bled.

Several SUA fled the onslaught of white phosphorus hellfire by stampeding through the door at the back of the car. James was waiting for them with his S&W M-76 SMG, catching his opponents as fast as they appeared in an impenetrable web of 9 mm destruction.

The Chicago hardcase had expended more than half of his subgun's 36-round magazine when the flow of SUA gunmen suddenly ceased. It was easy to see why. With a pile of bodies blocking the exit, anyone not making it to the door was already frying and dying inside the car.

Steel screeched against steel and the train began to slow, then stopped altogether. Cautiously, James climbed down from his perch as the flames lit by the M-34 grenade started licking through the passenger-car windows.

"Couldn't happen to a nicer bunch," Katz commented as he joined James on the ground and alongside the tracks.

They turned as Encizo and Narong approached from the direction of the locomotive.

"Everyone okay?" Encizo asked.

"So far as we know," said James.

"What do you suggest we do with the train?" Narong inquired.

"I think the fire will decide that for us," Manning said as he and McCarter hopped down from the small platform at the front of the caboose. "So much for the big delivery to the distribution center at Khao Soon."

Narong smiled. "I am sure it will be missed."

"What about Chang and the others?" Katz asked.

"Evidently, Chang killed off his partners shortly after we attacked," Manning said.

"And what happened to Chang?" James wanted to know.

McCarter grinned. "He must be dead. There's no way he could escape that inferno."

CHANG CHI-FU TOOK one final look at the burning wreckage and then turned and made his way back along the track. He knew his time was yet to come.

# 4 FREE BOOKS
# 1 FREE GIFT
## NO RISK
## NO OBLIGATION
## NO KIDDING